YOU THROW LIKE A GIRL

ALSO BY RACHELE ALPINE

Operation Pucker Up

YOU THROW LIKE A Girl

RACHELE ALPINE

ALADDIN

New York London Toronto Sydney New Delhi

ALADDIN

An imprint of Simon & Schuster Children's Publishing Division
1230 Avenue of the Americas, New York, New York 10020
First Aladdin hardcover edition February 2017
Text copyright © 2017 by Rachele Alpine
Jacket illustration copyright © 2017 by Dung Ho Hahn
Also available in an Aladdin M!X paperback edition.
For information about special discounts for bulk purchases, please contact Simon & Schuster
Special Sales at 1-866-506-1949 or business@simonandschuster.com.
The Simon & Schuster Speakers Bureau can bring authors to your live event.
For more information or to book an event, contact the Simon & Schuster Speakers
Bureau at 1-866-248-3049 or visit our website at www.simonspeakers.com.
Jacket designed by Karin Paprocki
Interior designed by Mike Rosamilia
The text of this book was set in Fairfield LT Std.
Manufactured in the United States of America 0117 FFG
2 4 6 8 10 9 7 5 3 1
Library of Congress Control Number 2016939166
ISBN 978-1-4814-5985-3 (hc)
ISBN 978-1-4814-5984-6 (pbk)
ISBN 978-1-4814-5986-0 (eBook)

TO NOLAN,
MY GREATEST ADVENTURE

IT WAS THE FIRST DAY OF SUMMER VACATION.

Mom called it the Summer of Girls.

My nine-month-old sister, Ava, called it, "Wah, Wah, WAAAAAH!"

And I called it the Summer without Dad.

But the truth was, no matter what you called it, this summer was going to stink.

How could it not, when I was trapped in a car, eight hours into a journey that was taking me far away from my friends, and a week ago we said good-bye to Dad as he started a year deployment overseas in a place thousands of miles away?

Save ME PLZ!!!!! I texted to my best friend, Maddie.

Come back PLZ!!!!! she texted back, and I wished I could.

We crossed the Indiana border and passed a giant sign that proclaimed Ohio THE HEART OF IT ALL. Mom beeped the horn three times. I sunk down in my seat to avoid the confused looks of the people in the cars next to us.

"Please, stop that," I told her, but my protests didn't matter. Mom beeped every time we entered a new state.

"How else am I going to announce to everyone that we've arrived?" she asked.

Ava thought it was hilarious, cooing each time Mom laid on the horn. I, on the other hand, wanted to disappear, from embarrassment. Especially when we'd crossed from Illinois into Indiana and Mom's horn had startled the guy to the right of us. He'd shaken his fist and mouthed some words Ava was definitely not old enough to learn.

"Are we there yet?" I asked for what was probably the fiftieth time that day.

"Not much longer," Mom said, which was the reply she gave me every time I checked. I had a feeling that if I had asked her the same question shortly after we'd pulled out of the driveway, she would've still said that it wouldn't take much longer.

I opened my mouth and let out a huge yawn. "This drive stinks," I announced, but no one bothered to answer, so I rested my head against the window and watched the world fly by.

We usually took a plane to Grandma's house, but this year we took the minivan. Mom thought driving would be an adventure that would help us bond. "Picture it," she'd said when she'd told me the news. I'd been lying on a folding chair in the backyard, soaking in the first day of warm weather and dreaming about the last day of sixth grade. "It'll be the three of us girls and the open road. We'll have so much fun!"

I'd told Mom I'd give it a chance, but I wasn't convinced this would be as "fun" as she believed it would be. So far my summer had consisted of nothing but endless fields, with the occasional farmhouse and cows. I was so bored that at one point I tried to count the yellow lines on the road, which didn't work, because Mom always went over the speed limit and it was all a blur.

We drove on, and another half hour ticked by, and then fifteen more minutes. I watched the world slip past outside the car window as we moved further and further away from our house and closer and closer to Grandma's.

Mom pulled off the highway, and we began to take side roads. I was one more winding road away from getting carsick when Mom pointed out the window.

"Gabby, look, we're getting close. There's LaMarca's Farm." One of my favorite sites to spot on the way to Grandma's house came into view. It was a two-story-tall corn statue that stood at the entrance of the biggest farm in the area.

I'd never been so happy to see a giant ear of corn. It meant we'd made it. Buildings and streets began to look familiar, and I felt a tiny flutter of excitement. We'd visited enough times in the summer that it kind of felt like my home away from home.

"Coneheads has orange swirl ice cream today!" Mom announced as we passed a small building painted with rainbow colors whose sign had a face with a cone on the top of its head like a hat. It was one of our favorite places to go when we visited Grandma, and who could blame us? Their chocolate chunk mint ice cream was the best I'd ever had.

We drove through the tiny downtown with a bunch of stores and restaurants, and passed under a giant banner stretched across the street that advertised the Corn Festival.

It had a countdown box announcing that there were sixty-one days until the annual event. Mom and Dad always made sure to time our yearly visit so we could go. It was a weeklong celebration with games, carnival food, rides, concerts, a beauty pageant, and most important, the championship game for the summer league softball and baseball teams. It was such a fun week. Everyone was in a great mood as they celebrated their biggest crop . . . corn! Mom said this year would be even more of a big deal because it was the fiftieth anniversary of the festival, so the town planned to waste no expense to make it as grand as possible.

We left the main stretch of town and passed the recreation center, which was full of kids at the pool. But I didn't care about the pool; it was the baseball field I was interested in. I watched a group of boys around my age playing a game, and I imagined myself on the pitcher's mound. Mom had promised me I could join the softball team here, and I couldn't wait to get out on the field and throw the ball around. But my good feelings evaporated quickly as I thought about how Dad wouldn't be able to watch me play this summer.

The car turned down Grandma's street, and the empty

feeling deep in my stomach became worse. Usually when we turned onto her street with the rental car my parents would get at the airport, Dad would drive super-slowly on purpose, which made me crazy, because all I wanted to do was race out of the car and jump into her pool. It was the best part of her house. I'd begged Mom and Dad for years to get a pool like Grandma has, but there was no budging them, so I made sure to get lots of swimming time in when we visited.

Today was different, though. Mom didn't drive slowly. She didn't remember the joke Dad would play, and for the millionth time that day, I wished he was here. I couldn't help thinking about him. How could I not? Mom said that I needed to keep my mind busy with other things so I wouldn't miss him as much, but that wasn't working at all. For either of us. I'd caught her a few times staring off into space with a sad look in her eyes, and I was pretty sure it was because she was thinking about Dad.

"I know this is hard on you; it's hard on all of us," she'd say. "But this summer will be good. I need help with Ava, and you'll be so busy making new friends that you won't even notice your dad is away."

But she was wrong. I'd never forget that he wasn't

with us. It'd been a week since we'd said good-bye to him, and we hadn't heard from him yet. Mom said that as soon as he was able to, he'd contact us, but waiting was the worst ever, because I had no idea if he was okay or not. I didn't say any of this to Mom, though, because I needed to be strong for her so she wouldn't get upset. Dad had told me to try to do that, and I wanted to make him proud.

I wiped my hands on my shorts and gripped the handle of the door. Even if Dad wasn't here, I couldn't break tradition. I was ready to get out of this car and jump into the pool. It was a ritual Dad and I had followed for years. We'd wear our bathing suits under our clothes, and before we even brought our bags into the house, the two of us would go for our first swim together. Mom and Grandma would sit on the porch with glasses of lemonade full of ice cubes, while Dad and I raced each other in the pool. We'd swim until our fingers were wrinkled like raisins and Mom told Dad to get out so he could start grilling. Even then, the two of us would eat at the picnic table in our bathing suits, not showering and changing until the sun had dipped deep down behind the trees.

Mom beeped the horn one last time as she pulled

into the driveway, and I was out the door before she even turned off the car.

"I'll bring my suitcase in later," I shouted, and ran away before she could protest. I pulled my shirt off over my head and wadded it into a ball. I ran around the side of the house, wiggled out of my shorts, and threw them onto the back deck.

I held my hands out and spun around, breathing in the familiar scent of fresh-cut grass and chlorine from the pool. As much as I didn't want to come here for the whole summer, it felt good to be back, and maybe, just maybe, things wouldn't be so bad.

I thought about what Dad would want me to do, took a few steps backward, and then ran forward and, with a giant cheer, did a cannonball into the pool. Summer had officially begun! When I surfaced, I swam to the other side by myself, pretending Dad was right alongside me.

IT WAS TOO COLD OUTSIDE TO STAY IN THE POOL LIKE
we would in the hot July sun. I swam for about ten minutes before my ears hurt when I wasn't underwater and
goose bumps spotted my skin. I jumped out and ran to
Grandma, who sat with Mom and Ava at the patio table.
Grandma looked the same, with her white hair curled
around her face and her blue eyes shining through her
red-rimmed glasses, which she says she wears to add a
little bit of sass to her wardrobe. She was familiar, and
familiar felt good right now.

I gave her a big giant wet hug. That's the great thing
about Grandma; she didn't even care that I soaked her.
She wrapped her arms around me and hugged right back.

"I'm glad you're here, kiddo," she whispered. "Life couldn't be better now that I have you for the whole summer."

I nodded and took a deep breath. Grandma's recognizable scent of oranges and something spicy filled my nose. At least some things were still the same.

After a few moments together, I stepped away from her and we laughed at the big spot of water that was now all over the front of her.

"I'm going to change into warmer clothes." I grabbed the towel she had set out on the chair and walked through the patio doors that led to the family room. The walls were covered with pictures of Mom when she was younger, most of her in the silly frilly pageant dresses she used to wear when she competed. She looked the same as she did back then, tan with a bright white smile and strawberry-blond hair that curled slightly on the ends. The only difference was that Mom now had wrinkles around her eyes and mouth. She was still pretty, and I could see why she'd won tons of pageants. Along with the pictures of her, Grandma had added a bunch of our family. Dad's face smiled back at me from a picture of the four of us we took after Ava was born, and my heart ached for a moment as I wished he were here.

"Strong, steady, strike," I whispered. It was the phrase Dad would say to himself back when he played ball, a mantra I copied when I pitched.

I hurried past the pictures and went upstairs to the room I always stayed in. But my suitcase wasn't there. Ava's duffel bag with the ladybug print sat on the bed.

Grandma came up behind me. "Not what you expected, right?"

"Mom put my suitcase in the wrong room."

"Your mom and I thought it would be a good idea to put Ava in the room next to her. That way Mom can get to her easily at night."

"But I always have this room." I tried not to show her how upset I was. I loved this room, with its tiny window that looked out over the pool. The ceiling slanted down, so if you were tall like Dad, you had to duck when you walked over there. I used to pretend it was my hiding spot, since I was the only one short enough to fit.

"We thought it would be fun for you to stay in your mom's old room," Grandma said, leading me down the hallway. She opened the door, and sure enough, my suitcase sat on the bed as if I had already agreed to the switch and there was no reason I'd have a problem with it.

"Thanks," I mumbled, not wanting to seem like a baby for getting upset about where I stayed, even though I most certainly was.

"Come down when you're changed; I want to hear all about what you've been up to this year."

I nodded, and when Grandma closed the door, I fell back onto the bed, even though my swimsuit was still damp and I'd probably get the sheets wet. I looked around the room, at the ceiling that didn't slope down, a vanity with a mirror that had lights all around it, butterfly drawings taped to the wall, and Mom's old pageant sashes and crowns on a bookshelf. I thought of my own room back home, covered with pictures of my favorite baseball players and the medals I'd won in softball. Both of our rooms might be filled with awards, but Mom and I couldn't be more different.

"So what do you think?" Mom asked, coming through the door. "It's going to be great staying in my old room, isn't it?"

She was so excited, I didn't have the heart to tell her how disappointed I was.

"It's great." I played with my bathing suit strap.

"I love that you're sleeping in the same room I slept in when I was your age. But guess what the best part is?" Mom asked.

"What?" I asked.

"Check out what's in the closet!" Mom pulled some plastic bags out and laid them on the bed. "My old pageant dresses!"

I groaned like I always did when she talked about her beauty queen days, but she ignored me like she always did and pulled one out. It was glittery and poufy and something I'd never ever be caught dead wearing.

"What is that dreadful thing? Quick, kill it before it attacks us!" I yelled, and fell onto the bed dramatically.

Mom put the dress up to her and twirled around the room. "Oh, be quiet. It's beautiful. I remember how I couldn't wait to wear it. And now that we're here for the whole summer—" Mom started, but I interrupted, because you didn't have to be a genius to know where she was going with this.

"Not going to happen," I said. I imagined myself in one of her dresses, and almost laughed out loud. I wasn't exactly what you'd call beauty pageant material. I'd look ridiculous in it, with my brown hair that I always wore back in a ponytail, perpetually skinned knees, and the arm muscles I have from pitching. I stood up and dug around in my suitcase, then pulled out one of my old softball T-shirts. "This is the only thing you're going to find me in, so don't get any ideas about me putting on one of your old dresses."

"Are you sure?" Mom asked, and pulled a dress out of the closet that was even worse than the first. It was hot pink, satin, and had giant shoulder pads guaranteed to make me resemble a linebacker.

I was used to her trying to convince me to wear her dresses. In her eyes, they were amazing because she was a real-life beauty queen. As in, Mom had won in all three age groups in the Miss Popcorn pageant during the Corn Festival. She's the only girl to have ever won the Triple Crown. She's a regular celebrity in town, and part of the reason we planned our yearly visit during the festival was so Mom could relive the past.

"You know, just because you like to wear T-shirts doesn't mean you can't ever wear a dress from time to time," she said, but I shook my head.

"The only thing I want to put on is a softball uniform," I told her. "I need to focus on my pitching. I promised Dad I'd pitch in the Corn Festival championship and help our team win."

Mom might have won all the crowns, but it was Dad's trophies I loved. Just like Mom was famous all over town for the pageant, Dad was legendary in town for baseball. He'd taught me everything about the game. The two of us would spend hours in the yard practicing pitching. We'd been doing that for as long as I could remember. And now that he was serving overseas, my goal for the summer was to pitch in the championship game like he did when he was my age. It might sound silly, but I felt like if I was able to do this for him, he'd come home safely.

"Dad would be so proud of you," Mom said. "And you're right. If you want to focus on softball, then that's what you should do."

"Thanks," I told her, so glad to have a Mom who supported me no matter what it was I wanted to do. She might not understand why Dad and I loved playing ball so much, but she always cheered me on in the stands at my games. She did this thing where she could put two fingers into her mouth and produce a whistle so shrill, I was pretty sure people the next town over could hear.

But as she put the dresses back into the closet, she lingered over them for a little longer. She was still dreaming about seeing me in one of those dresses, but that was one dream she was going to strike out on.

3

AFTER MOM LEFT, I CLOSED THE CLOSET DOOR, WHICH

I had a feeling she'd left open just in case it might persuade me to do the pageant, and I changed into some dry clothes. I dug through my suitcase and pulled out the hat Dad had given me the day he left.

You'd think the day your dad was deployed overseas would be a big event. He deserved a parade that marched by the front of our house with people cheering. A marching band should have played and the crowd should have held up giant signs with his name on it. Because after all, he was leaving his family to fight for the freedom of everyone else's families.

But the morning Dad left wasn't anything like that. We

had to get up at the crack of dawn, so early that the moon was still faint in the sky, and instead of having a family breakfast, Mom drove through the drive-through at McDonald's and Ava cried the whole way to the military base.

We checked in with security and pulled up to a plain brown building. There were lights on inside and a few cars parked in the lot, but no one was around, and I wished again for a giant send-off. We climbed out of the car but didn't go inside. We huddled together in the cold early-morning chill and tried to pretend Dad wasn't leaving us for a year.

When it was time for him to say good-bye, he kneeled down so he was on my level, and I tried my hardest to be brave, which didn't work well because I was crying.

"I'm going to miss you, Curveball," he said, using his nickname for me. It was my best pitch, the one Dad said I threw better than him. I wanted to tell him how much I'd miss him too, but all I could do was nod and keep back my sobs. I needed to be strong for everyone.

He reached into his bag and pulled out his faded baseball hat from college. It was his prized possession; he'd worn it all four years when he was their star pitcher. He'd had minor league scouts watching him, and Mom said he would have played with the pros if he hadn't enlisted after 9/11.

"I thought you could keep this safe for me," he said. He placed it on my head and stepped back to take a look.

I reached up to touch it. "For real?"

"It's the perfect fit," he said. "And when I come home, you can tell me all about the strikes you pitched."

Dad wrapped his arms around me and hugged so hard, I thought I might pop. But I didn't care, because once he let go, it would be time to say good-bye for real.

"I'm going to miss you like crazy," I whispered.

"Same here, Curveball. I'll be thinking of you every minute of every day."

Ava let out a high-pitched wail and reached her pudgy little arms toward Dad.

"I haven't forgotten about you," Dad said, and took my sister into his arms. "You better make sure you don't grow any new teeth or start talking until I get back. I can't miss out on all the important stuff."

She giggled as he tickled her under her chin.

Dad picked up his bag, and his mood turned serious. "I'm going to miss my girls like crazy."

He kissed each one of us and then headed to the

building's front door. He waved before going through and disappearing.

I still missed him today as ferociously as I had the day he said good-bye. I stood in front of Mom's fancy light-up mirror and put Dad's hat on. I stared at myself and promised that I'd do whatever I had to in order to make sure I pitched in the championship game.

I HAD TO WAIT THREE DAYS BEFORE I COULD OFFICIALLY become a member of the city of Chester's softball team.

Three whole days!

It might not sound like a lot to most people, but because I hadn't played since last summer, those days felt like the longest of my life. I was itching to get back on the field and throw some strikes to make Dad proud. And finally I'd be able to do exactly that. Today was the rec center's summer program information day. You were able to pick up your uniform, schedule, and roster. I couldn't wait to see what color my team shirt was. I hoped it was something cool like turquoise. Last year we were gray with white lettering—super-boring and not fun at all.

I was not a morning person, but today I woke up before Grandma had even started to brew the stinky coffee she makes, which had a smell that filled the house. My early wake-up was a pretty big accomplishment, especially since most mornings Mom had to yell at me multiple times and threaten to douse me with cold water to get me out of bed.

I pulled my hair into a ponytail and put on my lucky knee-high socks—the red-and-blue-striped ones, Cleveland Indians colors. I wore the socks all the time now. So much, in fact, that the right foot had a tiny hole where my pinkie toe stuck out. But I'd never get rid of them. They were the pair I'd had on last summer when I'd struck out five hitters in a row. Dad had watched in the stands and cheered so loudly that even the parents who had been there for the other team couldn't help but smile at how happy he was for me.

I found Mom getting Ava ready for a bath.

"Can't you do that later?" I asked, because I couldn't wait any longer.

"I'll be quick," Mom said as she put bubbles into the tub, but that wasn't true. Ava loved baths and always pitched a fit when it was time to get out. She'd stay in the water all day if she could.

"What if I picked up my team's information by myself?" I asked. The field was close enough to Grandma's house that I could ride my bike. "I've ridden there before with Dad to practice pitching."

"That doesn't seem safe," Mom said.

"Please," I begged. "You know how important this is to me."

And she did. While Mom would love for me to be interested in frilly dresses and beauty pageants, she understood how important softball was to me. And she especially understood how important softball this summer was. She knew about the promise I'd made to Dad to pitch in the championship game, and while she might not have understood my obsession with the game, I knew she'd do whatever she could to help make sure I got to pitch.

"You have to cross Benson Avenue."

"I'm going into seventh grade. I can handle it. I'll be super-duper-careful and make sure I use the crosswalk and traffic light when I get to Benson."

"Okay, okay, go ahead, but call me if you need me. And make sure you're back in an hour."

"I will! Thanks!" I rushed out of the house as fast as possible in case she changed her mind.

Before I climbed onto my bike, I sent a quick text to Maddie:

2day is the day! Picking up uniform and getting team schedule!!!!

Woo-hoo! They R lucky to have you! she sent back, and it felt like she was right there with me, cheering me on.

I rode to the park with a big grin on my face. I probably looked like an idiot, but I didn't care. I was on my way to play ball, and it felt amazing. One of the hardest parts about coming here this summer was that I left my team behind. Most of us had played together since we were seven, and the thought of a whole season without them was awful. Maddie and our shortstop, Coleen, cried when I told the team the news, which made me cry all over again. Maddie was the catcher, and when the two of us played together, it was next to impossible for a batter to get a hit. Our team called us the Dynamic Duo, and just the thought of breaking us up had made me feel awful.

Dad had been able to see how down I was, and had said it might be good to play with new people and see what I could learn from them. I hoped he was right, because at the moment all I felt was sweaty palms at the idea of meeting a whole bunch of strangers who had probably been teammates forever.

There were already a few long lines of parents and kids outside the rec center, so I left my bike against the trees and stood behind one of the groups waiting in front of the tables.

"Is this where you get your baseball information?" I asked two boys around my age who were having an intense argument about the new third baseman for the Pittsburgh Pirates.

"Yeah," one of them said. "But you're supposed to be over there."

He motioned to the line to the left of him. I raised my eyebrow, a bit skeptical. They had separate lines for boys and girls? And while the boys in this line wore sneakers and shorts, the girls in the other line seemed out of place. They were dressed in skirts and sundresses, and not one of them had sneakers on. One girl even wore heels, and another had her phone out and fixed her lip gloss using the screen. They weren't exactly sporting the athletic look, but I guess if you were here to pick up your uniform, then you didn't need to dress the part.

"Okay, thanks." I moved to that line. A girl with long blond hair that looked like she'd spent all morning curling it turned and studied me, as if sizing me up. She had on a short ruffled skirt, and her nails were painted bright pink. They were perfect, and I had no idea how she didn't mess them up playing ball. I thought of my own short nails with the polish flaking off.

I grinned and stuck out my hand. Might as well try to make friends, right? "Hi, I'm Gabby."

"Jessa," the girl said in an annoyed voice, as if she expected me to already know that. She ignored my outstretched hand and tilted her head to study me. I tried not to squirm, but I felt an awful lot like one of those worms we had to dissect in biology. "I haven't seen you before. Are you new?"

"I'm here for the summer," I told her. When she continued to stare at me as if something was wrong, I tried to explain. "My dad is deployed overseas, and we're staying with my grandma so my mom can have some help with my baby sister."

"Interesting . . . ," she said, but it wasn't in a nice way, more like she was mad at me for being here.

I thought about my team back home and how we

wouldn't act like this with someone new. They sure did things differently around here.

"So what's your talent?" she asked.

"My talent?"

"Yeah, what are you good at?"

Now I was completely confused. Was talent what people called your position here?

"Well, I'm usually the pitcher, but I'm also pretty fast at running the bases. What about you?"

Please don't let her pitch, I thought, because she certainly didn't give off the vibe of the type of girl who wanted to share.

"Um . . . okay." She looked at me as if I had grown a third eye. She turned around and began to talk to a girl near her that had on a ton of eye shadow and bright red lipstick.

"Is Jessa giving you trouble?" a short girl with red hair and freckles asked. She was dressed more casually, in white shorts and a green tank top. She smiled, and I decided she was the type of person I wanted to be talking to, unlike Jessa. "Jessa hates any type of competition, so don't take it personally. I'm Erin, and I'm glad you're here. It's about time we had some new blood."

"Thanks," I told her, relieved to have someone on my side. I wanted to ask Erin if she was on my team, but before I could, the line moved forward and two spots opened up at the tables. An older woman with big hoop earrings that swung when she moved her head gestured at me.

"What age group are you in?" she asked when I walked up to her. Unlike Jessa and Erin, she didn't find anything special about me being new. In fact, she seemed pretty bored with me.

"I'm twelve years old. Is that what you mean?"

"Okay, the preteen group. What's your name?"

"Gabby Ryan," I told her.

She paused and studied me in almost the exact same way Jessa had. What was it about people here? Hadn't their parents ever taught them that it wasn't polite to stare?

"Ryan," she said. "Is your dad Mitch Ryan? And your mom is Rose?"

"Yep, the baseball and pageant stars of the 1990s," I told her, because I was used to people asking that when we were here.

She let out a squeal of delight. "Oh, honey, this is

perfect! I used to be in the pageant with her. You'll have to tell her Marin Dasinger says hi. I'd love to catch up with her one of these days. And look at you! All grown up and competing in the pageant now too. This is fabulous!"

She grabbed a big green folder from one of the bins and handed it to me. "Have your mom fill these papers out and drop them off by the end of the week. All the information and requirements are in there, but I'm sure your mom will be an expert on everything. We'll have one practice before the Corn Festival starts, to run through everything and answer questions."

"Oh, no." I held up my hand in a stop signal. "I'm not here for the pageant. I'm here to get my softball stuff."

"Softball stuff?" she asked, puzzled.

"The summer rec book my grandma got mailed to her said we received our uniforms and team schedule today."

"There isn't a softball team this year," she said, as if that was totally normal and not the worst thing I'd ever heard.

"Whoa, whoa, whoa, wait a minute. What did you just say?"

"The rec center had a few girls sign up, but not enough for a team. Probably because it's the fiftieth anniversary of the Corn Festival, everyone is pageant obsessed. There isn't enough interest for softball."

"Not having a team is un-American or against the law!" I told her. I was all worked up, but I had the right to be. This was awful! It was horrible! How would I pitch in the championship game? Tears pricked the backs of my eyes, and I blinked fast, trying to keep them in so she wouldn't think I was a huge baby.

"We talked with Riverside, and they agreed that any girl who wants to play can join their team."

Play for Chester's biggest rival! Was she crazy? That would be like living in Cleveland and cheering for the Cubs in the World Series. You don't do that. Didn't she have any idea about loyalty? Playing for Riverside would be worse than not playing at all. I could imagine Dad's face when I told him I wasn't pitching for the city of Chester but for Riverside. That wasn't even an option.

"Or you could do the pageant instead." She dangled the packet in front of me. "How about I sign you up? We can always find a spot for Rose's daughter."

"Yeah, I don't think—" I started, but she wasn't listening. She pushed the folder into my hands and waved to the girl behind me to step up to the table. I moved out of the line as the next girl practically ran over me, a cloud of lilac-scented perfume trailing behind her.

"Your mom is going to be thrilled," Marin called out. "And wouldn't it be something if you won too?"

I didn't even bother to reply, because what does a person say when all of their dreams are stomped on and destroyed?

"This is horrible," I moaned, and it was. It truly was. I was mad. No, scratch that, I was fuming.

I got on my bike and pedaled so fast, I swore I saw smoke coming out of my tires. It was bad enough Dad was gone and I'd had to leave my teammates for the summer, but this, this was a trillion times worse.

It wasn't until I was almost home that I realized that while I'd spent all my time being angry about the lack of a team, I'd forgotten one important fact.

I'd let myself be signed up for the Miss Popcorn pageant.

5

I THREW THE FOLDER ONTO THE TABLE WHEN I ARRIVED home, and stomped up the steps to my room, vowing not to think about the stupid pageant again. It wasn't like I was going to enter the competition. No way, no how.

I mean, I liked to wear skirts or dresses, and it was fun to put on a little makeup when Mom allowed it, but that was a whole lot different from parading across a stage and smiling so big, you could see all of my teeth, which I could never picture myself doing.

I examined myself in front of the mirror. I wasn't like those girls who had stood in line today and waited to sign up for the pageant. I'm not bad-looking, with brown hair a little past my shoulders, Dad's hazel eyes, and lashes so long that Mom always says I'll never need mascara. I imagined myself all made up with a spray tan and fake nails like on those ridiculous TV shows Mom watched, the ones were the little girls get so dressed up, they look more like dolls than people. I stuck my tongue out at myself; I'd never be caught dead on a TV show like that. Instead I grabbed Dad's baseball cap and plopped it onto my head.

I picked up the photo I'd brought of Dad playing baseball in middle school and stood in front of the mirror. I curled my lip and squinted exactly like he did in the picture. It was my most fierce game face—the look I was the most comfortable in, the one that suited me.

I pulled my hair up and tucked it under his hat. The face that stared back at me could have totally been a younger version of Dad. In fact, with all my hair hidden under the hat, someone could even mistake me for a boy.

Wait a minute.

That was it!

That was my solution!

Maybe I could play ball for Chester this summer after all!

I ran into the family room, where Grandma kept her computer, logged on, did a quick search, and scribbled down a phone number on scrap paper. I closed my bed-room door with a soft click and punched the number into the phone, with my heart thumping in my chest.

"Hello. Chester rec center. This is Mandy speaking," a bored-sounding woman said.

"Hi," I started, and then coughed, changing my voice to sound deeper. "I just moved here and wondered if it was too late to sign up for the baseball league?"

"Not at all," she said. "What age group would you be in?"

"The twelve-year-olds," I told her, trying to sound calm, even if I felt anything but.

"Great. They practice on Wednesdays at four p.m.," she said. "Give me your name, and you can drop off your payment and pick up your shirt Wednesday."

I paused. "My name?"

"I need it to sign you up," she said, as if it wasn't entirely odd that I was hesitant about giving it to her.

What exactly should I say? I couldn't very well give her my real name.

"Um . . . Johnny," I told her. "It's Johnny Lofton," I repeated, trying to sound sure. It was the names of two of Dad's favorite players from when he was younger, Johnny Damon and Kenny Lofton.

"Are you sure?" the woman asked, and laughed a little.

"Yep, I'm sure. It's just, now that I'm twelve, I've been thinking about going by 'John,' since it sounds a bit more mature."

"Well, John/Johnny Lofton, you're all set for Wednesday."

"Okay, thanks," I said, and if she were in front of me, I'd probably have put my arms around her and hugged her. I hung up and pumped my fist into the air. I was going to play ball!

Wait.

I paused and let the reality of it all sink in.

I was going to play ball.

As a boy.

This was crazy!

I stood in front of the mirror again in Dad's hat. What had I gotten myself into? Could I really do this? And not the athletic part; I was positive I could play with the boys. Dad first taught me to pitch overhand and still had me practice using a baseball instead of a softball. The real question was whether I could act like a boy. I had no idea if I could pull it off, but if it was the only way I could play for the city of Chester this summer, I had to at least try.

As I examined myself in the mirror, Mom barged in

with the biggest grin on her face that I'd seen since Dad had left.

I yanked his hat off quickly, but she didn't pay attention to what I was doing. Instead she waved around something in her hand.

It took me a moment to realize what it was, but when I did, I understood my mistake immediately.

It was the Miss Popcorn pageant folder.

The folder I'd left lying on the table right out in the open so that it was easy for Mom to find.

Shoot.

"You didn't tell me you signed up for this," Mom said, her eyes bright and shiny.

"Actually," I started, and hated to burst her bubble of happiness. "It's kind of a funny story—"

"You're right. It is," she interrupted. "I missed your dad like crazy today, and then I found this. It was like a sign telling me I could keep busy by helping you prepare. This is exactly what I needed to take my mind off everything."

I watched Mom in horror as she gushed on and on about how happy she was that I was doing this. So it was impossible to say no, not after she told me how it made her feel.

Think, think, think, I told myself. My mind spun as I tried to come up with a way to get out of this, but all my good ideas had been used up for the day.

"We'll have to start practicing right away. We need to figure out a talent for you, find a dress, go over possible hairstyles, schedule some spray tans . . ." Mom ticked off a whole list of items that sounded worse and worse. She held the folder up in the air. "How about I fill these out today and drop them off? I'd love to see who is judging and catch up with some of my old friends."

"It's a bad idea. I'm not beauty pageant material," I told Mom, hoping she'd understand.

Nope. She didn't. Her smile disappeared and she got that faraway sad look she'd been getting on her face more and more often.

"Then why did you sign up for it?" she said, her voice quiet.

As much as I hated the thought of being in a pageant, I hated it even more when Mom got like this. And I guess maybe it was possible. Maybe I could do the pageant and play baseball. It was worth a shot, if it made Mom happy.

"No, you're right," I said. "I thought it would be hard to juggle competing with baseball. And I have no idea where to even start when it comes to training for a pageant. But I shouldn't be nervous, because I have the best teacher around."

Mom let out a thrilled laugh, and I felt a lot better. It had felt like forever since I'd seen her this happy about something. I didn't even say anything as she whistled the Miss America theme song and pulled out her awful pageant dresses again.

I WAS DEEP INTO A DREAM ABOUT PITCHING DURING
the World Series when a bright light shined in my face.
Someone had opened the curtains. I pulled the sheets
over me, but they were too thin to block out the sun.

"What is this cruel, cruel joke?" I yelled.

"Rise and shine, sweetheart," Mom said in a voice
too cheerful for this early in the morning. "Time to get up
and moving. The early bird gets the worm!"

I pulled the sheet down slightly and squinted at the
numbers on the clock. Six fifteen in the morning. Way
too early to be waking up in the summer, which is exactly
what I told Mom in my grouchiest voice.

"You can't sleep the day away, especially not when we

have work to do. Now sit up and drink this." She thrust a cold glass of some nasty-looking green drink into my hand, and I didn't have a choice but to sit up or have it spill all over me.

"What is this?" I eyed the glass suspiciously.

"A breakfast smoothie," she said in a voice way too enthusiastic for a drink that was the same color as the pureed peas-and-carrot medley that Ava loved. "It'll wake you up and give you the energy we need for our morning workout."

I put the drink on my nightstand and tried to convince myself this was a bad dream, but when I closed my eyes, shook my head, and then opened my eyes again, she still stood before me. In a hot-pink jogging suit, to be exact. If there was one thing I could say about Mom, it was that she never did anything quietly. She was always loud, both in how she acted and in what she wore. Dad said that's why he fell in love with her in high school, because you couldn't ignore her.

"I'm doing my own kind of working out right here in bed. I'm working out my sleep skills," I said, but she wasn't buying it. She yanked the covers off me, and unless I wanted to lie in the cold chill of the morning with the sun shining in my face, my time in bed was over.

"Okay, okay, geez, I'm getting up," I told her.

"And drinking that." She nodded at the drink next to me.

I picked it up and inspected it with distrust. It resembled sewer water. I wished I could plug my nose when I drank it, like I used to do when I was young and had to take medicine. I silently counted to three and took a big gulp to get rid of the awful drink as soon as possible. I waited for the nasty taste to hit my taste buds, but the thing was, it wasn't bad. In fact, while it might have been a yucky green color, it tasted kind of good, like bananas and strawberries. I took another sip, and Mom gave me a smug look.

"I told you that you'd like it," she said. "It's the breakfast of champions. Beauty champions, that is."

I groaned. "Is that what this is about?"

Mom nodded. "The first thing we're going to do is a morning jog. We don't have much time until the pageant, so we need to start training."

"What does going for a jog have to do with preparing for the pageant? It's not an athletic competition."

"Fresh air and some mother-daughter time is exactly what the two of us need. We can talk strategy, and afterward we'll stop at Newman's Bakery and get those blueberry bagels we love."

"That doesn't sound too bad," I said, and it didn't. Mom and I hadn't had time alone with each other since Dad had left, and jogging could count as conditioning for baseball.

Baseball. My stomach dipped a little when I thought about what I'd done yesterday, but not the bad kind of dipping, more like the about-to-go-down-a-big-hill-on-a-roller-coaster kind. I couldn't believe I'd lied and signed up as a boy, but it would all be worth it, because I'd get to play ball again.

"Great. Get dressed and I'll meet you downstairs."

I grabbed a shirt from the top of my hamper to go with a pair of shorts that sat on my chair. I couldn't say I was thrilled to go jogging, but it would be nice to spend time with Mom. And she couldn't talk about the pageant the whole time, right? Maybe we would even talk about Dad. Since he'd left, we'd never talked about him.

Mom was at the sink cleaning out the blender when I made it downstairs. I could see Grandma by the pool playing with Ava. I wondered if Mom had made Grandma a smoothie and had Grandma liked it? Mom probably had to convince her to take a sip too; Grandma was like me. We ate foods we could identify and that were normal colors.

"Ready when you are," I told Mom.

She turned and made a face at me. "Really, Gabby? You're going to wear that shirt?"

I glanced down at my purple-and-white-striped shirt. "What's wrong with it? I had it on yesterday and you didn't say anything."

"Exactly." Mom pointed to the top left side of it. "You had it on yesterday when you dropped that blob of ketchup on it."

I rubbed at the spot as if I could make it disappear. "It's not a big deal. We're jogging; it'll get sweaty anyways."

Mom adjusted her ponytail, which was already perfect, and shook her head. "You're a pageant girl now. You always have to be prepared to run into someone important. Go back upstairs and put on some clean clothes."

It wasn't worth the battle when it came to clothes. I'm pretty sure she ironed her workout gear, so this stained shirt would never fly with her. I changed without arguing and met her on the driveway, where she was stretching. It was still early, too early, but the sun was already heating up the day.

The two of us fell into a slow jog, and after my muscles warmed up and got used to running, it felt good to be outside. We ran through Grandma's neighborhood and down a tree-lined stretch of road. Everything was quiet, probably because the lucky people inside the houses were still asleep. Their newspapers waited at the ends of their driveways, and sprinklers made slow clicking sounds as they watered the lawns. I looped up onto the grass at one house and ran through the sprinkler, letting the water cool me off.

We cut up another street and were passing a yellow house with ivy growing all over the front, when the front door flew open.

"Well, I'll be. If it isn't Rose Brandis," a woman with bright red hair said in a high shrill voice, using Mom's maiden name.

"Molly Seifrick! I can't believe it's you!" Mom ran up the driveway and threw her arms around the woman. They both hugged and squealed at each other like they were my age instead of adults. The two finally let go and took a few steps back.

"It's Molly Whalen now. But look at you, Rose. You haven't changed in the last twenty years."

"Well, I'm not so sure about that. I'm Rose Ryan

now," Mom said, but there was no doubt she liked the compliment. "I could say the same about you."

"We still have it," Mrs. Whalen joked. I inspected this woman to see exactly what it was her and Mom still had, and while I wasn't sure, I was pretty sure they did both share it. They were practically twins, from their brightly colored workout tops and yoga pants to the perfectly styled ponytails and makeup even though they were dressed to exercise.

Mom turned to me as if just remembering I was there. "Things have changed a bit since I last saw you. This is my daughter, Gabby. Gabby, Mrs. Whalen and I did pageants together."

"And your mom won every one of them," she joked. "I never stood a chance."

"Pleased to meet you." I extended my hand, figuring Mom would be happy I used my manners like a true pageant girl.

"Aren't you the cutest," Mrs. Whalen said, and I tried not to cringe. "Cute" wasn't exactly the word I wanted people to use to describe me. I'd rather be athletic, tough, or strong. Words that meant something to me. "I have a daughter right around your age. You two should meet."

"That would be great," Mom said. "Gabby could use some friends while we are here."

"Let me go grab her." Mrs. Whalen turned toward the house.

"Oh, no, you don't have to," I said, because being set up by your mom's friend so that you'd have a friend was beyond embarrassing. But before I could stop her, she waved her hand at me like it was no big deal and ran into the house.

"I can't believe I ran into Molly," Mom said to me while we waited. "We had such a good time together when we did pageants. You're going to love all the girls you meet this year."

"We'll see," I told her as I thought about Jessa.

"Here she is," Mrs. Whalen said in the same loud voice I'd begun to assume was how she always spoke. She pushed her daughter forward as if she were presenting her, which probably embarrassed the other girl as much as it did me.

"Erin!" I said, recognizing the girl who'd stood in line next to me at the rec center.

"Hi, Gabby!"

I watched as our parents exchanged a confused look.

"You know each other?" Mom asked.

"Oh yeah," I said. "We go way back."

"Back to pageant sign-ups," Erin added.

"Well, this is great!" Mrs. Whalen said. "You can be pageant buddies like the two of us were. And what would be better than to get tips and secrets from the famous Rose Ryan?"

"I'd love that!" Erin said.

And I would too. Erin seemed like the type of person I could definitely be friends with. I was happy to see that she wasn't dressed up either. She had on a plain pink T-shirt and jean shorts. I resisted the urge to point out to Mom that not everyone dresses "pageant-ready," as she liked to say.

"Yes, that would be great," Mom said, because that's the type of person she is. Instead of wanting to keep all her secrets and tips for me, she was willing to help out her friend's daughter. And that was quite all right with me. If Erin and I prepared for the pageant together, Mom wouldn't focus all her attention on me. And Erin didn't take it as seriously as Jessa and some of the other girls that were in line with us, so it might be fun to prep together.

"Thank you so much for helping Erin," Mrs. Whalen

gushed. "It's not every day you get tips from a Triple Crown winner."

"This is going to be so fun!" Erin said, and the crazy thing was, I agreed with her. Maybe there was a little pageant girl in me after all.

I'VE NEVER BEEN A PATIENT PERSON. I HATE WAITING
for my bread to toast in the morning, I usually burn my
tongue on hot chocolate because I never let it cool, and
I peek at the last page of books to see how they end. So
it was no surprise how antsy I was the next day, waiting
for four o'clock to come around. Nothing helped pass the
time, and believe me, I tried everything, even helping
Grandma dust the house. But finally, finally it was time
to go to baseball practice.

I searched my suitcase to find the perfect outfit. Mom
kept bugging me to unpack, but it was easier to dig through
everything. Why would you want to waste time putting
away something you were simply going to pull out again?

I found the shirt I was searching for, the gray one from the team I played on last year. As I changed into it and some athletic shorts, I wondered what Maddie and my old teammates back home were doing. They'd started practicing the week before, shortly after I'd left. I bet Turah took over as pitcher. She always stepped in when I needed a break. Would the team accept her as the new pitcher, or did they miss me and wish I was still there? And what about our outfielder Khalia's little sister, Josephine? She loved cheering me on when I was in the groove and throwing strikes. I'm sure they were just fine without me, but a little part of me was sad if that was the case. I didn't want to be so easily replaced.

I needed to stop thinking about my old team and focus on my new one. This was my next great adventure, and I had to get moving, or I'd be late.

I grabbed Dad's baseball hat and my glove, and stuffed some hair ties and bobby pins into my pocket. The plan was to leave the house looking like a girl, but once I made it to the baseball field, there was a playground nearby, so I could duck into the bathroom and transform without anyone seeing me. The plan would work. It had to work.

49

I texted to Maddie, First day of practice. Sooooooo nervous!

They will LUV U! she replied, and it helped to know Maddie had my back.

Mom was in the kitchen feeding Ava as I set out to leave. My sister was fussing and spitting her food right back out.

"I totally get how you feel," I told her, looking down at the bowl of yellow goo. "I wouldn't be eating that stuff either."

"You sure you don't want me to take you to practice?" Mom asked.

"No," I quickly replied. "I was fine riding my bike there to pick up my information packet, and if I go myself, you don't have to interrupt Ava's delicious meal," I told her, wrinkling my nose at the food.

"Good, more for us," she joked, as she tried to get Ava to eat another bite. "Be careful and have fun."

"I will," I told her, and it was the truth. I hopped onto my bike and pedaled as fast as I could, because the playing field was calling, and I couldn't wait to get out onto it.

8

THERE WERE THREE GIRLS IN THE BATHROOM AT THE

park when I walked in, and it didn't look as if they planned to leave anytime soon. They brushed their hair, put on lipstick, and talked a mile a minute about some birthday party they'd all been to.

Great.

I slipped into a stall and waited for them to finish up and go gossip somewhere else. Finally after five minutes they left in a fit of giggles.

I bolted out of the stall and to the sink. I wasn't sure when another group of girls might come in, so I needed to make this transformation happen fast.

I turned on the faucet and wet my hair, slicking it

back into a sleek tight bun. I reminded myself more of a ballet dancer than a baseball player, but when I put Dad's cap on, you couldn't tell I had long hair. I took the eye black stick and made thick lines on my cheeks to block the sun and look tougher. I curled my lip and glared at myself in the mirror as if I were sizing up a batter. And the amazing thing was, I really did look like a boy. This might truly work!

"What do you think, Johnny?" I asked the face that stared back at me. "Can I fool them?"

I closed my eyes and pictured Dad cheering me on in the stands, as he had for so many games in the past.

"Strong, steady, strike," I told myself. I grabbed my bag, pushed open the bathroom door, and headed across the field. It was time to play ball!

9

IT ALWAYS TOOK ME A WHILE TO GET USED TO NEW people, so as brave as I tried to tell myself I was for joining the boys' team, I was terrified as I approached the bleachers. What if someone found me out? Then I wouldn't be able to play baseball this summer. If that happened, what would I do about the promise I'd made Dad? A million thoughts swirled around in my head, which just made me more nervous.

I clutched my glove against my stomach and gave myself a pep talk. "This is baseball. You love baseball. You're good at baseball. You can do this."

A bunch of boys sat on the bleachers, and more were dropped off from a line of cars in the parking lot. Some of them talked or joked with each other, a few threw balls into the air, and one cracked sunflower seeds in his mouth and dropped the shells into the space below the bleachers. I walked up the steps, conscious of my cleats clanging against them. My heart flipped in my chest and I held my breath, certain someone would instantly figure me out.

Usually I would've given a little wave or introduced myself, but that wasn't what I did today. These were boys, and I had no idea how to act around them. So I nodded at the group and sat down, put my feet on the bleachers in front of me, and rested my glove on my knee, copying some of the other boys.

And guess what?

No one gave me a look as if I didn't fit in. I let myself relax. If this had been a group of girls, they probably would have been sneaking glances at me and whispering—the pageant sign-ups helped confirm how an outsider was treated. But here, right now, all these boys couldn't care less about me. From their conversations, they were more interested in the batting averages of major-league players and whether or not some kid named Carlos would return this summer to play.

Except that I was wrong. The blond-haired boy with a big gap between his two front teeth studied me intently. My skin broke out in goose bumps despite the heat. Had he figured me out?

I summoned all of my courage and gave him my best scowl—I had to be tough, right?

"What are you looking at?" I asked, and tried to make my voice sound gruff.

He met my stare head-on and gestured at my hands.

I glanced down and felt sick to my stomach. My nails were covered in bright pink polish. How stupid could I be? I wasn't even five minutes into practice, and I'd already blown my cover. My dreams of playing baseball started to evaporate, unless . . .

"Oh yeah, my little sister. I babysat her the other night, and it was the only thing that would shut her up. I have no idea where my mom keeps the stuff you use to take this off, and I wasn't about to search through all her girly things. You never know what you might find." I made a face as if the thought of going through Mom's bathroom cabinets terrified me.

He made a face similar to mine. "That's the worst. I have two older sisters and avoid the bathroom they share at all costs." He nodded at my shirt. "Is that your old team?"

"Yeah, I'm here for the summer. I'm Johnny."

The name, surprisingly, felt natural, like it fit, and when he told me his name was Owen without questioning me, this felt like something I just might pull off.

After a few more minutes, a man around Dad's age stood in front of us at the bottom of the bleachers. He wore sunglasses with bright orange sides, had dark spiky hair that he ran his hand through as he talked, and had a goatee. He introduced himself as Coach Marshall and had us all come onto the field.

"I want to see you catch some grounders. Line up, and when I hit to you, field the ball and throw it to first."

I joined the line of boys and tried not to make eye contact, so none of them would look at me too long and discover my secret.

Each person ran up and did the drill, until there were only two in front of me. They both went, and then it was my turn. My knees felt wobbly, like the Jell-O salad Grandma always made when it was too hot out to cook. I could do this, I tried to convince myself. I was good at this. I was born to play baseball.

"Strong, steady, strike," I whispered as I crouched down in position to field the ball.

Coach Marshall hit a ball a little to the left of me, but I remained behind it and scooped it up and threw straight at first, where Owen caught it in his glove.

I jogged to the base to relieve him, and when the next boy threw the ball to me too high, I jumped up and caught it.

"Nice save," Coach Marshall yelled. I calmly nodded at him like I'd seen the other boys do, but inside I was freaking out. Because I was playing baseball and rocking it. And not just for a girl but for a boy, too!

WHEN I ARRIVED HOME FROM PRACTICE, THERE WAS A
buzz of excitement in the air that didn't have anything
to do with baseball or the pageant. Mom, Grandma, and
Ava sat on the front step as I rode up on my bike. I'd
pulled my hair out of the ponytail and looked like Gabby
again, which was a good thing. I had no idea what Mom
would do if she caught me dressed as Johnny.

Mom played peekaboo with Ava while Grandma
husked a big bag of corn for dinner. "How was your first
practice?" Mom asked. "Did you have a good time?"

"The best time! It felt great to throw the ball around
again." I stuck to a general response, so that I wouldn't tech-
nically be lying to her. And it was the truth. Practice had

been great. We'd done a few more drills and then split into two teams and scrimmaged. Coach Marshall let me pitch for three innings. I struck out four people, and when I was up to bat, I made it onto base twice. There were boys on the team who didn't even get on base once, so if anyone figured out I was a girl, it wasn't because of the way I played.

"Your dad will love to hear that," Mom said.

"He would," I agreed, and felt a swell of pride.

"You'll have to make sure to tell him about it tonight."

"Tell him tonight? What do you mean?"

"Oh, just that I received an e-mail that he'll be able to video chat with us in a little bit."

"He will?" I shouted so loudly that Ava looked up, startled.

Mom picked her up and held her high in the air. Ava let out a happy squeal, mimicking Mom's good mood. "He will, so why don't you run upstairs, take a quick shower, and change so you don't miss talking to him."

"Oh, I won't! I'd never miss out on that." I couldn't believe it; I was going to get to talk to Dad. This was the best news ever, and I couldn't wait to tell him about my first practice. I took the stairs two at a time and didn't even wait for the water in the shower to heat up before I jumped in. I showered in record time and afterward stood in my bedroom, stumped. I had no idea what to change into. But while I might not have known the answer, I knew someone who would.

"What's up?" Mom asked as she peeked into my room after I called her. She had on a sleeveless blouse, flowing skirt, and lipstick, but that didn't help, because Mom was always dressed up.

I stood there still dripping from my shower and gestured toward my clothes. "What exactly should I wear to talk to Dad?"

Mom took a look at me before answering my question. "Well, you certainly aren't going to talk to him in a towel."

"Ha-ha," I said.

"Put on something you feel comfortable in. Be yourself. You don't want Dad thinking he went away and you changed into a totally different person." I agreed with her, but when she left, I thought back to today's practice, and the irony of her comment wasn't lost on me.

I pulled out my favorite pair of jeans and tank top with sparkles on it. It was nice but not too fancy. I was halfway down the steps, when I turned and headed back to my room. I grabbed Dad's hat and placed it on my head. I caught a look at myself in the mirror as I headed back out. Perfect. Now I looked like myself.

Everyone was gathered around Grandma's computer. They didn't even lift their eyes from the screen when I walked in. So I pulled up a chair and joined them.

We watched the minutes change at the corner of the computer screen. When it was three minutes past the hour, Mom began to fidget. At seven past, she shook her head.

"I don't think he's going to call," she said, and her voice sounded so sad that I wanted to crawl up into her lap like I used to when I was little and tell her everything would be okay, but I was nervous too.

"Relax," Grandma said. "He told you he'd call around six. There are probably other people using the computer and he has to wait his turn."

"That must be what's going on," Mom said, and I saw her glance at the clock again.

At eleven past the hour, the computer made noise and a strange number flashed on the screen.

"It's him, it's him!" I shouted, and wiggled in my seat. "Answer it," I told Mom.

She pushed a button, and Dad's face filled the screen. We all cheered when Dad waved, and suddenly Dad didn't feel so far away.

"Hello!" his voice boomed out of the speakers, and

we crowded around, answering him back. He laughed and held up his pointer finger. "Okay, okay, one at a time."

"Hi, Dad," I shyly said when it was my turn.

"Hey, Curveball," he answered back. "How has life been treating you?"

"Good," I told him, because I didn't want to say anything negative. He'd told me to be brave for Mom, and that's exactly what I planned to do.

"Are you playing ball?"

"Yep, I joined the team and had my first practice today. I struck four people out when I pitched."

"I bet you're the best girl on the team," he said.

"You could say that," I told him, leaving out the fact that I was the *only* girl on the team. He didn't need to be bothered with minor details, right?

"I'm so proud of you," he said, which was weird. Dad was the one we should be proud of—he served overseas to protect us, but it did feel good for him to say that. It helped make what I had done seem like the right thing. Maybe I had lied to people and fooled them, but was it so wrong when the reason was for someone else? Especially when that someone else was Dad?

MOM AND I CONTINUED OUR MORNING JOGS, AND THEY
weren't all bad; it was nice to spend time with her, with
the added bonus of a blueberry bagel at the end.

This morning we decided to take a different route.

"It's time for a bit of a challenge," Mom said. "Let's see
if we can tackle some of those hills we keep avoiding,"

I gulped down my smoothie and slammed the glass
onto the table. I held my arms up and made muscles.
"Bring it. Those hills don't stand a chance after my supercharged morning drink."

"We've got this!" Mom agreed, and after stretching out on the driveway, the two of us fell into a steady

pace as we left Grandma's neighborhood and took a left instead of our usual right.

Well, we "had" this for about ten minutes. But then our steps became significantly slower and my supercharged energy was soon lost.

"I'm thinking that we might have to review our route in the future. I miss those smooth flat roads."

"I couldn't agree more," Mom said as she huffed and puffed.

My calves felt as if they were on fire, and the hills seemed more like mountains. I was about ready to call it quits when the ground finally evened out. Mom and I took the opportunity to walk and catch our breath.

"We've definitely earned our bagels today," Mom said.

"With extra cream cheese," I added.

We walked for a while not saying anything, just thankful for a break and a chance for our hearts to slow down.

The street we were on was pretty quiet, but up ahead I could see a boy washing a big truck. He finished spraying it down with a hose and dipped a giant sponge into a soapy bucket of water. Country music played from a speaker on the front porch, and a glass of water full of ice sat next to it. I seriously considered asking him for a drink if he looked up at us.

Mom waved, and I was about to do the same, until he looked up. I found myself locking eyes with Calvin, one of the boys on my baseball team.

"Morning!" Mom said, and his attention was diverted away from me.

I seized my chance. I didn't even think about it. I just ran. And not the running Mom and I had been doing earlier, but full-out Olympic sprinter running. I needed to get out of there, and I needed to get out of there fast. Because the problem was, I looked an awful lot like Johnny. My hair was pulled back into a ponytail under Dad's hat, and I had on my summer rec shirt that I had worn to practice a number of times.

The hills were a lot easier going down than they had been when we'd run up them, and I was moving so fast, I was surprised I didn't fall and hurt myself. I ran far away from his house, and then I ran some more. It wasn't until I reached Grandma's house that I finally collapsed in the soft grass. I was lying there stressing about my close call when a shadow fell over me.

I opened one eye and saw Mom standing above me

with her arms crossed and an incredibly angry look on her face.

"What exactly was that?" she asked.

I pretended to be asleep, but she wasn't buying it. "Gabriella Ryan, I asked you a question. Why did you run away from me like that?"

I shrugged, because the truth wouldn't work and there was no way I could convince Mom that I was now a long-distance runner.

"I saw a bee," I tried.

"And so you ran for over a mile to get away from it?"

"I had to. It was very aggressive. "

"Right," Mom said, and gave me a look as if she assumed I had officially lost it. "You have to be careful of those aggressive bees."

"You've got that right," I told Mom. "There's nothing worse."

But that was a lie. There was something very, very worse. Calvin finding out I was Johnny, but luckily, we were safe for today. And that's exactly the way I liked it.

THE NEXT MORNING I CONVINCED MOM THAT WE
needed a break after yesterday's run. And since Erin
planned to come over today, she miraculously agreed,
and when Erin showed up shortly after Grandma had
cleared the breakfast dishes, Mom took the opportunity
to share one of her smoothies.

"Wow, this is good," Erin said after she'd tried it. She
took another giant gulp, and Mom grinned, probably glad
to have converted someone who didn't put up a big protest like I did.

After Erin sucked her smoothie down in a matter of
minutes, she held up the bag she had brought.

"I have the heels I plan to wear in the pageant. My

mom told me you called her to make sure I'd bring them." Erin pulled out a pair of satiny white sandals with sparkly rhinestones across the straps. The heels were long and thin, like sharp pointy icicles just waiting to make her fall flat on her face. At least, that's what would happen if I wore them.

"Perfect! And those are beautiful!" Mom said, giving Erin her official pageant queen seal of approval.

"They look like torture devices," I said.

"Gabby, do you always have to be so dramatic?" Mom asked. "And I'm sorry to say, you're about to be tortured too, because I happen to have a pair for you."

She walked into the living room and came back with a shoebox that she placed in front of me.

"You better be joking," I told her, and cautiously opened the lid of the box as if a snake would jump out. And truthfully, I'd rather find a snake than the pair of black sandals that lay nestled on tissue paper.

"What do you think?" Mom asked. "I made sure to get some with a small heel."

"Any heel is going to be a threat to my life. I'll never be able to walk in these," I told her. Maybe it did have a smaller heel, but a heel was a heel. When you're counting on tiny toothpicks to hold you up, nothing feels safe.

She pushed them into my hands before I could even begin to protest. I looped my fingers through the straps and held them in front of me. They dangled like the worm Dad had speared my hook through when we'd gone fishing years ago. That was absolutely disgusting, and I pretty much had the same feeling now that I had then.

"I thought today we'd practice the introductions and how to walk onstage," Mom said. "You only get one first impression with the judges, so you want to make sure it's a good one."

"That sounds great!" Erin said with way more enthusiasm than I'd ever feel about this pageant.

"Not everyone can cross the stage with style and grace," Mom informed us. "But I'll show you how to do it."

I opened my mouth to tell Mom how silly it was to teach us to walk, but then I saw Erin studying Mom with intensity, ready to soak up everything Mom had to say. So with a big sigh I kicked off my flip-flops and put on the heels. They pinched my toes together, and I was pretty sure a giant blister had already formed. I swayed a little in them but regained my balance. Did people put these on for the first time and walk normally in them? Was that even possible?

"Perfect!" Mom said after I took a few baby steps. "Now let's head outside. It's a gorgeous day, and we can practice walking around the pool."

It took about five minutes for me to make it from the kitchen to the pool, because I had to move slowly and make sure I didn't wipe out.

Mom had Erin and me line up next to the diving board. She sat down in a purple-and-white-striped lawn chair and pointed across the water to the shallow end.

"Imagine the pool is the stage. You'll walk slowly along the side and stop once you reach the center. Stand up straight and be confident. Introduce yourself and share a few things you like to do. You'll have a microphone for the actual pageant, but today let's practice speaking loudly and clearly. Make sure you enunciate. I should be able to hear you from where I'm sitting."

Erin stepped back so I could go first, which is exactly what I didn't want to do, but she was a guest, so I had to be polite.

"Okay, ready," I told Mom, and struck a funny pose with my arms up in the air. I mean, after all, it wasn't like I had a chance of winning the pageant, so I should have fun with this and not think too much about it, right?

She ignored my goofiness and launched right into an introduction of me. "Our next contestant is Gabby Ryan." She spoke in an official-sounding voice that reminded me of a game show host.

I walked across the outside of the pool and tried to stand up straight like Mom had taught us. I couldn't move too fast because of the heels, but I thought I was doing pretty well. So well, in fact, that I put a little wiggle in my step and shook my hips. The judges must want personality, right? You didn't want to be a cookie cutter of everyone else, or how would they notice you?

I reached the center of the pool and stopped. I put my hands on my hips and enthusiastically said, "Hi. I'm Gabby Ryan, and I like to play baseball and swim. I recently started drinking green smoothies in the morning and found eating your veggies isn't that bad when they're blended with strawberries and bananas."

I waited for Mom to say something, but she remained silent. Erin, on the other hand, gave me a thumbs-up.

"Well . . . ," Mom finally said, drawing out the word. "That was certainly enthusiastic."

"Yep, that's what I was going for."

"You do want to show them who you are, but you

could do it in a little more of a . . ." She paused, as if trying to find the right word. "Reserved kind of way. The thing is, you want to still appear professional when you're up there. Save your personality for the talent portion."

"Professional?" I asked, ignoring her comment about the talent portion, because it was a tough subject between Mom and me. She was on my case about what I wanted to do, and no matter what I said, she absolutely refused to recognize throwing a baseball as a talent. She wanted me to sing or dance, two things that would get me laughed off the stage.

"Yes, remember the pageants we watch on television. You want to act as if you're being interviewed by the president of the United States."

"The president?" I asked, highly doubting she'd come to our pageant and help pick Miss Popcorn.

"You know what I mean," Mom said. "And keep in mind how you present yourself. You don't want to look sloppy."

I remembered the other morning when she'd made me change my shirt. She probably hated what I had on today too. My hair was in a messy ponytail, my shirt was a faded Cleveland Indians jersey, and I had dug the last clean pair of shorts from my suitcase. They were a wrinkled mess. My new heels most definitely didn't go with anything in this outfit.

"We're in the backyard; no one is going to be judging me."

"Erin took the time to get ready," Mom said, and I saw Erin squirm a bit. At least she didn't like being compared to me. But Mom was right. She had on a light yellow tank top with a white skirt. Her hair was pulled back into a headband. She looked like she tried, but not too hard. I'd never admit it to Mom, but I wouldn't mind asking Erin for some tips on how to look cute but not like you spent hours getting ready. "And you need to be careful. Those Band-Aids aren't going to look good when you're up onstage during the pageant in a dress."

"I'm proud of these battle wounds. They show I'm not a wimp and can be tough."

Mom let out a sigh so loud, I heard it from across the pool. I didn't care, though. She could sigh all day long. I wasn't about to be careful in baseball just so I looked good for the pageant. In fact, that sounded an awful lot like something one of those girly girls I met in line at the rec center would do.

"How about this?" I asked, and walked back to Mom in

the way she'd taught us. I stopped in front of her. "Hi. My name is Gabby Ryan, and I like to play baseball and swim." I spoke slowly and loudly, and when I was done, she nodded.

"Good, that's a lot better, but we should work on your hobbies. We want something more exciting to catch their attention. Something exotic."

"Exotic? I thought this pageant was about showing who I was, not trying to be someone else."

"I'm not asking you to change who you are," Mom said, and I swear I thought she was going to sigh again. Instead she turned to Erin. "How about you give it a shot?"

Erin glanced at me, and I rolled my eyes. She giggled and then walked the same length of the pool I had. She didn't go too fast or too slow and smiled in a way that was genuine, not like she faked it, which was what it had felt like for me. She was a natural.

"Hi. I'm Erin Whalen," she said when she reached the center of the pool. "I spend my afternoons playing golf with my dad or living out adventures through books, and on the weekends I volunteer as a dog walker at the animal shelter. When I grow up, I want to anchor the evening news and travel the world covering stories about important events."

"Now, that's the way to do it! " Mom said, and you'd think I'd be jealous of all the compliments Mom was giving Erin today, but it was the opposite. Mom would love me no matter how clumsy I was with all this pageant stuff, and now with Erin as part of her training, it would give Mom the chance to coach a potential winner. So it was a win-win for all three of us, because with Mom's attention on Erin, it would be off me, or should I say, it would be off Johnny.

"How about you try it one more time, Gabby, just like Erin did?"

"One more time," I told her, because if I didn't get out of those heels soon, my feet were going on strike. Why would anyone willingly make the choice to wear shoes like this? And how the heck did they wear them all day long? I'd take my sneakers over these in a second.

I gave myself a silent pep talk, took a deep breath, and walked around the edge of the pool as if I were born to be a pageant queen. I paused when I reached the middle, to give Mom my new and improved introduction. Except, right before I could, I leaned back too far back and lost my balance. I shifted my weight, but it only made it worse. I teetered back and forth, and the heels on my shoes made it impossible to steady myself.

75

I took a step forward, my foot twisted, and I fell.

Right into the swimming pool.

I made a splash so big, my talent could have been the cannonball.

The cold water shocked me, but I didn't mind. It felt pretty good after a morning of pageant practice in the hot sun. I swam to the surface and wiped the hair out of my face. My clothes stuck to me and felt heavy. Erin and Mom were at the edge, looking down at me with worried expressions on their faces.

"Are you okay?" Mom asked.

"I'm fine." I splashed some water up into the air to show her it wasn't a big deal. I floated on my back and wiggled my feet. "However, I'm not so sure about these shoes."

"Yeah, maybe we'll get you a cute pair of flats," Mom said, and laughed.

"That's one pageant tip I can agree with," I told her.

I pulled off the heels and let them sink to the bottom of the pool.

I CHANGED OUT OF MY WET CLOTHES AND PUT ON A
sundress, figuring it wouldn't hurt to make a little bit of
an effort.

Mom smiled when I came downstairs but didn't say
anything about my new outfit.

"I need to go into town and get some groceries. Do
you girls want to come with Ava and me? I'll drop you off
at Coneheads and pick you up on the way home."

Really? Did Mom even need to ask if we wanted ice
cream? And before lunch? This was a dream come true!

She turned the radio up real loud in the car, and the
three of us sang along, making up silly words for the
songs we didn't know. Even Ava joined in with her happy

babble, and it felt nice to relax and take a break from pageant prep.

It was only eleven thirty in the morning, but Coneheads was packed. I guess we weren't the only ones who thought it would be a good idea to have dessert before lunch.

"Your mom is so cool. First pageant tips and now ice cream," Erin said after we'd gotten our cones and sat down. "Thanks for letting me practice with you."

"Of course. I'm glad it's not just me and her crazy pageant tips."

"So about her pageant tips," Erin said, and then licked around the edge of her cone to catch the drips before speaking again. "It didn't make you mad that your mom made you practice everything so many times?"

"And you only had to practice it once," I said, because that was what she was getting at.

She shrugged. "Yeah, I wasn't that good. She was only being nice to me."

"Are you kidding? She loves helping you out. And you're good. This is the perfect situation. I'm not exactly living up to her expectations of what the daughter of a pageant queen should be, so you give her someone to prep to possibly win it all."

"You're doing great," Erin said, and I let out a little snort at how far off she was.

"Great for someone who never thought she'd be in a pageant. What about you?" I held my ice cream cone up to my mouth like a microphone. "Please tell the judges, Erin, why do you want to be Miss Popcorn?"

I turned the pretend microphone toward her, and she sat up and turned all serious. "Well, by winning the crown, I'll be able to spread world peace everywhere."

"Oh yes," I told her, and nodded my head enthusiastically. "World peace is very important and something that can definitely be accomplished by our next Miss Popcorn."

"What about you?" she asked, and pointed her cone at me.

"Well, when I'm not off doing exotic things, I dream about saving all the lobsters in the seafood restaurant tanks and setting them free."

"A very noble thing to do," she said.

We continued to ask each other silly pageant questions as we finished our ice cream, and when we got up to throw our napkins away, we made sure to do the most exaggerated pageant walk we could imagine. I swung my hips so far that I knocked into Erin, who was taking giant steps forward. The two of us dissolved into giggles.

"I'm glad you're here for the summer. It's good to have a friend like you," Erin said, and slung her arm around my shoulder.

I had to agree. I hadn't been sure I'd like it here after leaving my friends at home, especially when I found out there wasn't even a girls' softball team, but it was all falling into place, both with baseball and with Erin. And the strangest thing was that today I hadn't worried about Dad once. That had to count for something. I was about to tell Erin how glad I was to have met her too, when I heard a voice behind me.

"Well, isn't this cute."

We turned and found ourselves face-to-face with Jessa, who was dressed to impress, as Mom would say, in a polka-dot dress, giant white sunglasses, and platform sandals. I let out a little shiver as I thought about the heels I'd worn earlier. But unlike me, Jessa didn't appear to be in pain at all. How she walked in them, I had no idea, but from the way she moved closer to us, I had a hunch Mom would've said she had perfected the pageant walk. This girl oozed Miss Popcorn vibes.

"Hi, Jessa," Erin said, making the effort to be a lot more friendly than I would've been. Truthfully, Jessa kind of scared me. While I had no problem standing up to girls who hit home runs and players who stole bases, I had no idea what exactly to do with someone as stuck-up as Jessa.

"I couldn't help but overhear the two of you practicing pageant questions," she said.

"Oh, we weren't using questions the judges might ask. We were joking around," Erin said.

"What a relief," Jessa said in a nasty way. "For a minute there I thought the two of you believed you stood a chance."

"We didn't say that," Erin said, her voice a little less friendly.

"But it's the truth. Some people are cut out to be in the pageant." Jessa paused before she looked straight at me. "And some people aren't."

I put my game face on and glared at her. I imagined myself standing on the pitcher's mound staring down a batter when there were two strikes and three balls in the final inning, and suddenly Jessa wasn't scary. And I sure as heck wasn't going to listen to Mom's advice about being all sugar and spice and everything nice, because I wasn't about to let Jessa talk to us like this.

I stepped in front of Erin and tried to look tall and tough, even though Jessa probably still had a few inches on me, with those platform sandals. "Actually, we have it under control. My mom is teaching us the ropes. I'd suggest you find a coach too, although it might be hard to find someone as good as my mom. After all, she's the only one who has ever won the Triple Crown."

Jessa stood speechless, unable to answer back to that. I continued to stare her down triumphantly as her mouth opened and closed. She was at a loss for words.

"What's wrong? You can't find an answer?" Erin asked. "That wouldn't work well in the interview part of the pageant, now, would it?"

"That's not allowed," Jessa finally said. "Gabby's mom helping the two of you is an unfair advantage."

"Is it?" I asked, playing right into her words. "Well, then, I guess it's a good thing we aren't cut out for the pageant. That means we won't be a threat to you. Now, if you'll excuse us, we need to head home and practice our top secret pageant tips."

I grabbed Erin's hand and pulled her away from Jessa.

"Whatever," Jessa called after us. "All the help in the world won't prepare the two of you."

Erin and I ignored her; I turned to Erin and made a fist to use as my microphone. "The judges are curious, what would you do with a girl who clearly believes she already has winning the pageant in the bag?"

Erin grinned at me. "I'd make sure I did everything I could to beat her."

"And that response," I said, "gives you a perfect score of ten."

I QUICKLY BECAME A PRO AT DUCKING INTO THE
bathroom at the park and tucking my hair under my hat
to transform from Gabby to Johnny. Unfortunately, I
wasn't as good at keeping up the role during practice.

Owen had been my catcher the last few practices.
Ever since I'd told Coach I was a pitcher, he'd paired us
together. We were a good team, and I was glad to have
someone who wanted to work with the new girl. I mean,
the new guy. I hoped Coach Marshall would let us play
in a real game soon.

Today during warm-ups we practiced the signals for
my different pitches and fell into a pretty steady rhythm
of me throwing mostly strikes right into his glove. After

a particularly good changeup, he paused before tossing the ball back.

"What's wrong?" I asked.

"Why do you keep doing that?"

"Doing what?"

"After each pitch you touch the side of your hat with your hand, almost as if you're itching your ear."

"I do?" My hands instinctively moved up to my ears. They weren't itchy, so I had no clue what he meant.

He shrugged. "No big deal. It's just weird."

He threw the ball back and then signaled for me to throw him a curveball. I nodded, wound up, and let it loose.

"There! You did it again!" He caught the ball and then jumped up from his crouching position. He pointed at me as if he were accusing me of something. "What is that? A secret signal you're giving to someone?"

I dropped my hands back to my sides. I knew what was going on. I was tucking my hair behind my ears. Well, I would've been if my hair hadn't been slicked back to my head under my hat. When I pitched in softball, I wore a ponytail, but the motion of throwing the ball always made loose strands fall into my face. Loose strands that I brushed back after I pitched. Except, today I didn't have any hair to tuck back.

Quick, quick, quick, I told myself. What could I tell him to explain what I was doing? I couldn't very well use the truth.

A bee flew lazily past me in a clumsy circle. I jerked away from it and thought about how Dad would swipe at them when they bothered us. I was always scared they'd get angrier and come after us with a vengeance.

That's when I got my idea.

I waved my hands in front of my face again in a similar fashion to how I tucked my hair behind my ears. "Ugh, it's these flies. They're circling my head. It must be because of how bad I'm sweating. My mom's been on my case to wear more deodorant."

I shrugged my shoulders as if to say, *Mothers, what can you do about them?* but secretly I was mortified that I'd told a boy that I had a sweating problem. Especially when I didn't. I always made sure to put on lots and lots of deodorant, thank you very much.

"Oh yeah, I totally get you. My mom's the same about taking a shower after practice. She yells at me about sitting on the couch and stinking it up. But sometimes I want to relax, you know what I mean?"

I nodded like I totally understood what he meant, and fought the urge to gag at the grossness of it all. His mom had a point. I wouldn't want him getting my couch all sweaty and nasty either.

Thankfully, I was saved by the bell. Well, whistle.

"All right, boys. Let's gather round," Coach Marshall said, and signaled us back to the infield.

"We have our first game in three days, which means I need to decide who is going to play what positions. I may rotate you around a bit today when we scrimmage as I try a few ideas out, so don't get upset if you're not in your usual spot. But on the other hand, if you have a position you'd like to play, now is the time to try your best at it." He held up his clipboard and called out names. "All right, on team A . . . Ben, you're going to play first base. Jack, I've put you on second. Calvin, you're going to be our pitcher, and, Georgie, you'll catch."

He continued to assign other positions, but I didn't hear any of them after he told me I'd start as pitcher for team B. I grinned at Owen, who would be my catcher.

"Now is our time to shine," Owen whispered as we jogged to our spots. We were first up in the field.

"Let's show them what we've got," I told him with a

bit more enthusiasm than I felt. I was scared out of my mind, even more than I had been in fourth grade when I rode the Millennium Force at Cedar Point for the first time. This was my chance, and I had to get it right.

I took my spot on the mound and rotated my arm a few times to keep it warm. Coach Marshall went over the batting lineup, and the first few players were good. Matthew had even hit a home run the other day at practice, the ball sailing all the way over the fence and getting lost in some trees. Coach was definitely making me work hard to prove I had what it takes.

Owen signaled the pitch, and I nodded quickly at him and then looked the batter, Calvin, straight in the eye. It was something Dad had taught me. So many pitchers don't look at the batters, but his secret was eye contact. Force them to look at you, and don't break their gaze. Dad said it intimidated the batter and showed that you weren't afraid of anything. But today it was all an act, because I was terrified to pitch right now, since how well I did now would determine whether I pitched in real games.

However, I wasn't about to let Calvin see my weakness. So I pretended I wasn't afraid of a single darn thing and that he didn't stand a chance against me.

"Strong, steady, strike," I whispered to psych myself up. Dad's mantra calmed me a bit, and when I threw the ball, it whizzed past Calvin.

"Strike one!" Coach Marshall yelled, and Owen gave me a thumbs-up.

The second pitch was just as sweet, landing in the center of Owen's glove with a satisfying *slap*. Calvin swung and missed, and I fought back the urge to fist pump the air. I was two for two, and it felt amazing!

"You've got this!" AJ, our first baseman yelled, and I did. I totally had this.

Owen signaled at me to throw him a changeup. The perfect pitch for right now. Dad had taught me to throw it low and slightly to the right, so that it was hard to judge what kind of pitch it was. It was the type of pitch that made you swing because you were afraid it was a strike.

And swing Calvin did. And this time I did fist pump the air. Because I'd struck him out! One, two, three, straight in a row; he didn't even stand a chance!

Those first three pitches made me feel invincible, and I felt the familiar surge of confidence I remembered from playing on my team at home. I struck out two more batters and allowed only one run, which wasn't even my fault. William missed a pop-up that was hit right to him, and he had to chase after it. Coach Marshall pulled me out after four innings to give anyone else who wanted to pitch a chance, but I had a good feeling this wouldn't be my last time pitching.

"There was no getting past us!" I told Owen when we sat down on the bench to watch the next inning.

"We're a great team," he said, and I felt warm and fuzzy inside. I'd found Chester's version of Maddie here, and it felt pretty darn good.

"Great job, Johnny," a voice behind me said as I focused on Zach, who was on the pitcher's mound. No doubt hoping for the position.

Owen jabbed his elbow into me.

"Ouch! What did you do that for?" I asked.

He gestured behind me. "Calvin is talking to you."

Right, I thought. Johnny was me. *Get it together, Johnny, or you're going to blow your cover.*

"Sorry." I shrugged my shoulders at Calvin in apology. "Too focused on the game."

"No problem. You were great out there." He punched me on the shoulder in that way boys do, but the thing is, it hurt. Really hurt.

"Thanks, man." I resisted the urge to rub my arm. Instead I punched him back, but he hadn't expected it, and I caught him off guard. He took a few steps backward to regain his balance and gave me a funny look.

I felt my face heat up. Right when I thought I'd figured out how to act like a boy, I'd messed it up.

"So you pitched for your old team?" Calvin asked.

"Yeah, my dad taught me when I was young. He played college ball and couldn't wait to have a da—" I froze, shocked by what I almost said. "A son who played too," I finished.

"Well, he's a great teacher. I have a feeling Coach Marshall is going to make you our starting pitcher."

"That would be awesome." I felt a thrill of excitement race through me.

"How long have you been playing?" he asked.

"I've been on teams since I was seven. I've played with the same people for most of the time. I miss them, especially this season. My softball team is favored to be one of the best in the league, so it stinks that I won't be able to be a part of it."

"Your softball team?" Calvin asked, and I swear, if there was an award for putting your foot into your mouth, I'd be the hands-down winner today.

"We play with the girls sometimes," I said quickly. "We have to use a softball, since they don't pitch with baseballs."

"That must be interesting," Calvin said. I felt guilty for all of these stories I made up, but I told myself it was for a good cause. "I'd hate to play with a bunch of girls. They aren't exactly a challenge for us, are they?"

He laughed, and I joined in with him so he didn't get suspicious, although inside I was seething. I felt like a traitor. All I wanted to do was give him a piece of my mind. Girls were just as good as boys, and many times, even better. I thought about all the batters I'd struck out and vowed that the next time we scrimmaged and he was up, I'd do whatever it took to strike him out and show him exactly how weak girls were.

I heard the crack of the bat and saw a ball fly into the outfield.

"Yay, go!" I jumped up and shouted and clapped. I was done with this conversation. I continued to cheer at the top of my lungs, and it worked. Calvin left and headed to an open spot on the bench. I sat next to Owen and tried to calm down. Some people were so unbelievable, but it didn't surprise me in this town, a place where girls competed in beauty pageants instead of playing sports, and boys thought there was no place for girls on the playing field. What I didn't get was why it couldn't be both ways. Why couldn't girls play ball and compete in pageants? I giggled to myself; I guess it was possible. I was living proof of it, even if I was the only person aware that it was happening.

"Calvin's right," Owen said, and I felt another jolt of anger. Not Owen too. *You have to be kidding me.*

"Really? Because I don't believe it for a second," I shot back.

"You don't?" Owen asked. "Well, you should. Coach Marshall is going to make you starting pitcher. Zach didn't even come close to what you showed us on the mound."

A wave of relief rushed over me. Owen didn't mean girls not playing baseball. He was talking about me pitching. Thank goodness.

"As long as you're the catcher," I told him.

"Deal," Owen said, and with that, the two of us confirmed what would undoubtedly be the greatest duo in Chester, Ohio, history.

I CALLED MADDIE AS SOON AS I GOT HOME. THE TWO
of us never kept secrets from each other, and I felt guilty
for not telling her sooner about what was going on. Mom,
Grandma, and Ava had gone to the grocery store, so I had
the house to myself, which meant we could safely talk
without anyone overhearing.

"Please tell me your mom has decided that you're
all immediately coming back home," she said when she
answered.

"I wish," I said. "That would be the best ever. But so
is what I'm about to tell you."

"You're the youngest pitcher to ever get drafted into
the major leagues?"

I began to laugh and couldn't stop. That's the way Maddie was. She always thought the best of me, and I loved it. No matter how bad a mood I was in, she could make it better. It didn't hurt that she was able to make the funniest faces in the world and the best grilled cheese sandwiches I ever had.

"Not quite," I told her when I calmed down. "But it's about as crazy as that happening. Are you sitting down?"

"I am now, because I have no idea what you're about to say."

"Prepare yourself, because I'm pretty sure you're not going to believe me. Okay, so do you remember me talking about the Corn Festival that happens here?"

"Remember? It's all your mom talks about."

"True. So this year is the fiftieth anniversary, and pretty much every girl in the world wants to be in the beauty pageant."

"Except you, right?" Maddie said, and when I told her the story about accidently signing up, she was the one laughing uncontrollably.

"That's not the craziest thing." I told her about everything. And by everything I mean about Chester rec's newest pitcher, Johnny.

"You're unbelievable," she said. "But that's why I love you."

"Right back at you. Now tell me all about what you're doing. Is Ella still dropping the ball in right field? What about Bridget? Has she hit any home runs?" And the strangest thing happened as she filled me in on their season. I didn't feel the familiar pang of sadness that I usually did to be missing out on their season, because I was too busy playing ball here. And I had Johnny to thank for that.

THE NEXT MORNING I WAS SURPRISED TO WAKE UP
and see that it was almost nine. Mom had been barging
into my room for the last two weeks to wake me up for
our morning jog, so this was unusual.

I rolled over and snuggled into my pillow, savoring
the extra time to sleep in, but my mind wouldn't relax.
Why hadn't Mom come in this morning? Maybe she'd
overslept, but that didn't seem likely, since she was one
of those crazy morning people who have done a hundred
things already before you've even brushed your teeth. It
didn't make sense. She was way too into our daily jogs to
forget, so that could only mean something was wrong.
And that something could very well have to do with Dad.

I jumped out of bed and rushed downstairs. I tried to stay calm, but my brain wouldn't let me, filling my head with a whole bunch of "what ifs." *Please, please, please don't let it be Dad,* I chanted to myself.

I practically fell down the last few steps and raced into the kitchen, where Mom and Grandma looked at me in surprise. Ava happily smashed pieces of banana between her fingers and laughed. If something was wrong, they were doing a good job of hiding it.

"Whoa, slow down there. Where's the fire?" Mom asked.

"Why didn't you wake me?" I asked, and burst into tears.

"Sweetie," Mom said, and rushed over to me. "What's wrong?"

"You didn't come and get me. I thought something happened to Dad." I began to sob.

Mom wrapped her arms around me. "I'm sorry, Gabby. I wanted to let you sleep in today since we need to start practicing your talent. I didn't mean to worry you."

I let her stroke my hair as I tried to get myself under control. My body was shaking and my face was a snotty mess. "I was so scared," I whispered into Mom's chest.

"Everything is okay. Your dad is okay, and we're okay," she told me in a soft calm voice.

"How about I make some chocolate chip pancakes?" Grandma suggested. "That always puts me in a good mood."

"Instead of a smoothie?" I asked.

"Yes," Mom said. "Most definitely instead of a smoothie. We could all use some pancakes this morning."

So pancakes were eaten, and while I still missed and worried about Dad, it wasn't the overwhelming fear I'd felt earlier.

Things were all under control, until Mom ran upstairs to change and came back wearing some crazy spandex outfit with a sweatband around her head. She looked like a dancer on one of those old exercise videos she worked out to. But that wasn't the worst of it. Because in her hand she had a shiny silver outfit that shimmered in a way that promised to make anyone wearing it look like a giant disco ball.

"I have a surprise for you." She held the horrid thing out to me.

"My eyes, my eyes! They're burning!" I joked, and placed my hands over them.

"Ha-ha, very funny," Mom said.

"What is that?" I asked, looking at it as if it were roadkill.

Ava reached out her chubby hand and tried to grab it. She let out a happy scream, and Mom beamed at her.

"You like this, don't you, baby? You love Mama's old dance outfit she wore in the pageant. Maybe when Gabby is done wearing it, you can have it."

"I'm not wearing that," I said. "I'd blind everyone, and I'm not going to be held responsible for death by sparkles."

"Try it on. You might be surprised." Mom held it up against me.

I stepped away from her. It was even more hideous up close. The outfit had a ruffled top with long sleeves, and tiny shorts. Translation: nothing I'd ever be caught dead wearing.

"What exactly were you dancing to when you wore this? Circus music?"

"Really, Gabby," Mom said. "Can't you take anything seriously?"

"I'm trying to, but it's pretty hard to do when that giant neon eyesore is right in front of me."

"I give up," Mom said, and carefully draped the outfit

over the back of the chair, as if it were fragile. "Forget the outfit right now; we'll figure that out later. We need to focus on your talent and make sure it's perfect in time for the pageant."

"No worries. I don't mean to brag, but I'm the best pitcher on the team. I'll wow all the judges with my skills."

Mom wrinkled her nose as if she had smelled a carton full of rotten eggs. "Please tell me you really don't think you're pitching at the pageant."

"Why not? I thought I could stand at one end of the stage and throw to a target at the other. Maybe stack some bottles up or something fun that I could knock down. It'd be unique and get the judges' attention." I'd thought about this idea a bit, and while it was definitely different, it could be just the type of different the judges would like. They were probably totally bored of girl after girl either dancing or singing, so my talent could wake them up and give them a breath of fresh air, as Grandma liked to say.

"There's a certain expectation in pageants," Mom said. "Judges are looking for specific talents that can express your poise and grace. Pitching isn't one of those. When you're with your team, you get to show off your pitching, but when you compete, you want to demonstrate something better suited for the pageant. How about we learn a dance and then we can go from there? If it doesn't work, we'll figure something else out."

"I'm not going to be any good," I told her, but I didn't argue. Any mention of baseball these days put me on edge. Mom had been on my case more and more to come watch me pitch, which was something that most certainly couldn't happen. I told her that I wanted her and Grandma to wait until the championship game, so I could impress them with my skills. Mom was disappointed, but between pageant practice and taking care of Ava, I also think she was glad to have one less thing to juggle.

"I thought I'd teach you my old routine. How fun would it be to do the same number I did when I was your age and won?"

"I'm not so sure about that," I said, because if I had to dance, at least I could do it to some cool song I liked. "Wouldn't it be better to do something new?"

"No way, this is a great choice. It was a classic when I did it, and the judges loved it. I'm sure they'll feel the same with you."

Mom led me outside to where she had already set up

our "dance studio." She'd pushed back the patio furniture, and a CD player sat on the table.

"Whoa, we're even listening to the song in classic style."

Mom scowled at me. "I couldn't figure out how to download the song, and I found my old CD in my pageant box."

"More like 'time capsule,'" I said as I picked up the CD, and even Mom cracked a smile at that.

"Okay, let me show you the first part of the routine and you can repeat after me." She started the music and did a series of moves involving spins, twists, and a giant jump that even a prima ballerina would have trouble doing.

"I'm not sure . . . ," I said slowly.

"Give it a shot," Mom said. "I'll walk you through it the first time."

And she did. She also walked me through it the second, fifth, and tenth time, and I still couldn't figure it out.

"No, you need to turn right, not left," Mom said as I spun the wrong way yet again.

"I'm trying," I told her, and I was. I truly was. I couldn't help it that I stunk. Mom continued to slow down the choreography, and when I thought I had it down, I turned the wrong way again and hit my leg on the table.

"I quit!" I announced, and collapsed onto the ground. I felt a bit like Ava during her tantrums. The concrete of the patio was warm from the sun. I gazed at the pool and wished I could dive in and sit underwater, hiding from all of this. I wanted to do the pageant for Mom, I did, but it was obvious I wasn't cut out for it. When I couldn't do something in softball, I practiced, and it would get easier, but that didn't seem to be the case here. If anything, the more I practiced, the worse I became.

"Let's try it again; you'll get it," Mom said, but even she sounded like she was at her wit's end with me, and who could blame her? She probably wanted to call the hospital where I was born and tell them that she had received the wrong child at birth. She was an expert at pageants, so shouldn't I be the same way?

"Not today." I stood up and shook my head. "I'm checking out before I break a leg. Face it, this isn't happening. The only thing the judges will be doing when I'm onstage is laughing."

"That's not true," Mom said, but from the look on her face, I could tell she agreed.

"It is!" I yelled a bit too loudly as I headed inside. Ava, who was napping in her Pack 'n Play in the family room, woke up and began to cry. "Great! I can't even walk into the room without messing things up."

"Now you're being dramatic," Mom said as she picked Ava up and rocked her in her arms.

"Then maybe I should do a monologue for my talent!" I yelled, even though Mom was right. I was acting like a bigger baby than Ava was, but I wasn't about to admit that. I stormed out of the room and headed into the kitchen to get some water. Grandma was at the counter mixing something in a bowl.

"How did the practicing go?" she asked.

"It didn't," I told her.

"Want to talk about it?"

"Not really." What I wanted to do was go up to my room, climb into bed, pull the covers over my head, and try to forget the stupid dance I couldn't do.

"I have some cookie dough here with your name on it," she said.

"I'm okay," I muttered.

"Are you sure? It's peanut butter. We don't have to talk. You can sample it and make sure it tastes good."

"With chocolate chips?" I asked. I loved when Grandma put chocolate chips in her peanut butter cookies. They tasted like gooey Reese's Peanut Butter Cups.

"We can add them. They're in the cupboard above the oven."

I'm a sucker for her cookies, so I walked over and dug around until I found the bag. Grandma already had a spoon waiting for me with some cookie dough on it.

"Before you add those, how about you test the dough? It's always a good idea to try it with and without the chocolate chips."

"Multiple times, right?" I asked, and took the spoon from her.

"Of course." She pulled out a measuring cup and poured a bunch of chocolate chips into it. "So the dance isn't going too well?"

"I thought we weren't talking about it."

"You're right, you're right," she said. "I just know how frustrating the talent portion can be. Your mom struggled with it too when she was your age."

"She what?" I asked, and paused, my spoon about to dip back into the bowl for some more dough. Were we talking about the same person? Mom was super-pageant-woman; she was amazing at everything that had to do with competing.

"Your mom was born with two left feet. Totally uncoordinated. At her ballet recital when she was six, she headed one way while all the other girls went the other way. She froze and had no idea what to do, so she burst into tears and ran offstage. It didn't come as easily as she makes it seem. Believe me, there were plenty of meltdowns and hours and hours of practice before she got it right. We enrolled her in all kinds of dance classes—ballet, tap, jazz, but she couldn't get the hang of it. It broke my heart, because from the first time she saw the Miss Popcorn pageant when she was four, all she talked about was winning that crown."

"Mom wasn't born good? She ran off the stage?" I stared at Grandma in amazement. All of this blew my mind. "I assumed Mom was dancing up a storm in the hospital room when she was only a few minutes old."

"She eventually learned, but believe me, none of her pageant winnings came without hard work."

"She never told me that," I said, still not quite believing Grandma. Mom always made it look effortless.

"It's one of the rules of life. No one talks about the work involved or the negative stuff. They only focus on the positive, and for your mom that was when she finally figured out the dance and made it look easy. So remember that when you get frustrated. It usually isn't easy being good at something. Like all the hours you and your dad spend practicing baseball. "

"I'm not even sure years of practice will help me figure out that dance, but it helps to hear that Mom wasn't born flawless."

"No one is," Grandma said. "So give yourself a break. And finish scraping the cookie dough out of the bowl so I don't need to scrub it clean."

"If you insist!" I pulled the bowl over and slid my spoon around the edge, making sure to get every last bite of dough. Grandma put the cookie sheet into the oven and came back to me and put her hand on my shoulder.

"Don't worry about being perfect. Be yourself. That's what the judges want to see."

"I will," I said, but it was easier said than done. It felt like all I'd been doing these days was pretending—about not being scared about Dad, about wanting to be in the pageant, and about being a boy on the baseball team. I'd have loved to be myself, but the problem was, I wasn't even sure who the real me was anymore.

ERIN SHOWED UP AT MY HOUSE THE NEXT MORNING IN a hot-pink tracksuit.

Hot-pink.

"What are you doing, trying to become my mom?" I joked, but it didn't seem so far off. The two of them were pretty much becoming twins. Erin was a natural at pageant prep, and Mom was excited that at least one of us was able to use her self-proclaimed "Triple Crown Genius," as she so liked to remind the two of us when we goofed around and didn't take her seriously.

Don't get me wrong, it wasn't like Mom made me feel bad, but whereas Erin's "interview answers were magnificent," my interview answers were "coming along."

Or Erin's posture was "as good as the girls who are in the Miss Teen USA pageant," my posture was "better than yesterday." They weren't exactly insults, but it wasn't something I'd brag about either. Not that Erin ever bragged. I did the bragging for her. I told her over and over again she was awesome and Jessa better watch out, but Erin didn't believe me.

"I'm not a threat. I don't even care about the beauty part. I'm using this to prepare me to be a newscaster," she said as Mom had each of us walk around the pool with an egg on a spoon. It looked as ridiculous as it sounded, but Mom was a firm believer that this would help with our pageant prep, and Erin bought into it and slowly moved, while I, on the other hand, had already broken two eggs.

"It's all about moving slowly and steadily," Mom called out. "You don't want to drop the egg and have it break. Remember that when you're onstage."

"How about we take a break and scramble up these eggs? It's boiling hot; we could probably cook them on the concrete here," I complained, because I was done parading around with spoons. There was only so much I was willing to do for this pageant, and I'd pretty much reached my breaking point.

"It is heating up," Mom agreed, and fanned herself with her hand. "It's going to be a hot one today."

"We should go to the community pool," Erin said after Mom headed inside to get Ava up from her nap.

"Why would we go there, when we have the one right here?"

"Because it's where everyone hangs out. I'll introduce you to some of the people in my grade. It'll be fun."

The idea of going somewhere new did sound fun, and if I were back home, the pool is where I probably would be if I wasn't on the softball field. I agreed, and so it wasn't long before Erin's mom dropped us off and we waited in the line to get inside. There were a ton of people in front of us; it seemed like everyone had the same idea we did.

It took about ten more minutes to get into the pool and find a free spot to put our towels down. As soon as we did, I pulled off my shorts and tank top and waited for Erin to do the same.

"Hurry, hurry," I told Erin. "I want to get into the pool and cool off before the lifeguards blow the whistle for rest period."

"Relax. We have time," Erin said, and pulled out a bottle of sunscreen. She began to apply it, and I hopped from foot to foot as she covered pretty much every part of her. Finally she was done, but as we headed to the pool, the screech of whistles filled the air all around us.

"Rest period," yelled all the guards in unison.

"Nooooo," I moaned back.

"Sorry," Erin said, and she did look apologetic. "It's the redheaded curse. When you're as pale as me, you have to pretty much apply the whole bottle."

"It's okay," I told her, but stared longingly at the water as a bunch of adults dived in, able to enjoy the pool without all the kids. Would the guards let me go for a quick dip if I promised not to splash?

"Look on the bright side," Erin said. "Now we can go get some french fries. The snack bar here makes the best around."

"Isn't it kind of hot for fries?" I asked.

"It's never too hot for these fries," Erin said in a serious voice.

"I'll take your word for it." I followed her to the line for the snack bar, which was even longer than the one to get into the pool. It seemed as if everyone else around us stayed cool in their wet bathing suits, while we continued to bake in the sun.

"Hey, how about giving us cuts?" a loud voice said.

I turned and saw a boy with dark curly hair come up next to Erin.

"Get out of here," Erin said, and pushed the boy away. "You need to wait in line like everyone else."

"Oh, come on. Let us go in front of you," someone else said. The smell of chlorine and sunscreen filled my nostrils.

"Gabby, this is my annoying cousin, Andrew," Erin said, pointing at the boy who had come up to us first. "And these other guys are his equally annoying friends, Georgie and Owen."

I turned toward the boys to introduce myself, and stopped. Because standing with Erin's cousin were my teammates.

"Hi," I said quickly, and moved out of line to get away from them. I pretended to read the snack bar menu and that it was the most exciting thing in the world, so I didn't have time to talk to the guys.

"Gabby, get over here," Erin said, and pulled me back to the group. "Gabby is visiting from Wisconsin for the summer, so you all need to be nice to her."

"Wisconsin, huh? Does that make you a Brewers fan?" Andrew asked.

"No way. I only cheer for the Cleveland Indians," I said,

unable to resist showing my team loyalty, even if it meant bringing attention to myself.

"You're an Indians fan? Are you crazy?" Georgie asked, his voice full of disgust.

"They're the only team worth cheering for," I shot back, because no one was going to put down my team. Dad and I were die-hard fans. Dad would say that we could take him out of Cleveland, but we'd never take the Cleveland fan out of him.

"Obviously you haven't followed Cleveland's season. Because they're stinking up the division right now," Andrew said.

"That's because they're saving up their energy to come back and crush everyone," I shot back.

"Dream on," Andrew replied.

I turned to Erin and spoke in a loud voice. "I'm not so sure about your cousin. He might have gotten hit in the head with a baseball. He's delusional."

"Oh geez," Erin said. "You're a clone of Andrew and his friends. I thought I'd gotten away from baseball."

"It beats being pageant-brained," Andrew said.

"For your information, Gabby is competing in the pageant, so watch what you say."

"A pageant girl, huh? You don't act all girly," Georgie said, and I felt uncomfortable. I didn't want to talk about myself. And I didn't want to talk to the boys at all anymore.

"Oh shoot. I forgot to bring my money," I told Erin, even though I had a five-dollar bill clutched in my fist. "I'll be right back."

"Oh, don't worry," Erin said. "I have enough. You can pay me back."

I willed the line to move faster or for Erin to tell her cousin and the other boys that we weren't going to let them cut, but instead everyone focused their attention back on me.

"You look familiar," Owen said. "I can't figure out how, but I swear I've seen you somewhere."

"Yeah, Owen's right," Georgie replied.

"I'm not sure," I told them, and my stomach felt as if I was racing down a mountain on skis with no way to stop. I was sweating like crazy, not from the heat but from the fear of being found out.

"Where are you staying?" Georgie asked, trying to figure out how he recognized me.

I was sure they'd figure it out soon. It was a matter of time before they linked me to Johnny. I quickly took my hair out of its ponytail to cover more of my face, even though it made me hotter.

"Maybe you go to my church?" he asked.

"We haven't gone to church here," I told him.

"Hmmm . . . ," he said, not giving up his quest to blow my cover. I could practically see the wheels turning in his head as he tried to place me. I shifted from foot to foot, surprised the boys couldn't see how uncomfortable I was. "What about—"

TWEEEEEEET! "Rest period is over!" The lifeguards stationed around the pool yelled in unison.

"Thank goodness," I said, and without another word I got out of line, tucked my money in my backpack, and ran to the edge of the pool, where I proceeded to dive into the cool water. I swam until it felt as if my lungs would burst. I came up in the middle of the pool, took a giant breath, and dove back down again. I kicked as hard as I could. I wanted to get away from Erin's cousin and Owen and Georgie. Far, far away from them and their questions, before the group figured out exactly why they recognized me. I surfaced at the deep end of the pool and bobbed there, afraid to turn around and face the direction of the snack bar. I imagined the three of them lined up, shouting that I was Johnny.

How long could I stay here before I'd have to get out and face everyone again? Could I wait until the pool closed? Maybe hide out here until the pool emptied out for the night.

I was trying to figure out ways to disappear when a hand wrapped around my ankle. I screamed, and as I kicked myself loose, my foot connected with something.

"Ouch! That hurt, Gabby," a voice said.

I stopped thrashing around and saw Erin treading water next to me. "Sorry," I told her, feeling awful.

"What is up with you? Why did you run away like that when we were all talking?"

"I was hot; I needed to cool off. I seriously felt like I was about to pass out," I said, even though it was the lamest lie in the world.

"You were hot?" Erin asked. "I don't buy it. One minute you're there, and the next you're running away."

"Okay, okay. The truth is I'm kind of shy around boys," I lied, hoping she bought this excuse, so she wouldn't think I was a complete weirdo.

"Why didn't you say so? I'm the same way. My cousin's friends are annoying but nice, so you don't have to be nervous."

"Easier said than done, but I'll try to act normal next time I see them."

"As long as you promise not to run away again, then all is good."

"Promise," I said, because the odds of running into them again here was a big fat zero. This was my first and last trip to the pool.

MOM WAS OKAY WITH ME RIDING MY BIKE TO GAMES

and practices, and it worked out great for a couple of weeks, but then Coach Marshall changed all that with a single sentence.

"Tomorrow we play Perry on their field," he said to all of us as we sat around him after practice. "It shouldn't matter, though. You're all great players, so let's show the other team that we can't be stopped anywhere. What do you think? Can we do that?"

The rest of the team cheered their agreement, but I stayed silent, a sinking feeling in my stomach. I hadn't even thought about away games. Perry was almost fifteen minutes away by car. I couldn't very well ride my bike all the way there, and asking Mom to drive me was out of the question.

"What's wrong?" Owen asked.

"Nothing," I quickly said.

"I'm not buying it. You haven't said a word since we sat down, and you have a funny look on your face. Something isn't right."

"It's tomorrow's game. I didn't even think about playing in other cities," I said. I figured I might as well tell the truth, because I wasn't sure how else to answer. "My mom takes care of my little sister, so it's hard for her to drive me places. That's why I ride my bike everywhere."

"That's going to be a long bike ride. Perry is pretty far away. You should probably head out now if you want to make it in time for the game," Owen said, and I wanted to cry. This wasn't funny.

"Something like that," I said.

"I'm kidding. My dad can drive you. He watches all my games."

"Really?" I asked.

"Sure, it's not a problem. We'll swing by your house tomorrow and pick you up."

Um, yeah. That was going to be a problem. A big problem.

"That won't work," I told him, and he gave me a look as if I'd sprouted twenty heads.

"Okay," he said, and sounded as confused as I felt.

"It's just that my mom hates when people come to the door, because my little sister takes naps and if she wakes up, it's not good." I hated that I was building one lie on top of another, but I didn't know what else to do. "Maybe you could pick me up here?"

"That's silly. We'll make sure to be quiet. Don't worry about it. I know how cranky my mom gets when she doesn't get enough sleep, so we'll make sure not to wake your sister."

"Okay," I said, because what else could I do? I had no other solution, and if I kept arguing with Owen, I'd lose the only way of getting to the game that I had. I'd just have to hope I could slip out of the house easily without anyone noticing.

IT WAS AS IF THE UNIVERSE WAS LISTENING TO ME, because the next day, when Owen's dad was supposed to pick me up, Mom really was putting Ava down for a nap. I could hear my sister's cries, which meant Mom wasn't having a lot of success. I looked out the front window, my hand on my duffel bag so I was ready to go as soon as they arrived. I had tucked my hair up under my hat and told myself that I could quickly pull it out if I needed to.

Ava's cries were still loud and clear when a gray minivan pulled into the driveway, which meant I was free to make my getaway without being spotted. I stopped at the bottom of the steps and yelled upstairs to Mom. "I'm leaving for the game!"

I ran out the door before she could answer and slid into the minivan as if I were stealing second base. Both Owen and his dad looked at me in surprise.

"I'm here! Let's go play some ball!" I clapped my hands together and hoped they took the hint that we needed to get out of there ASAP.

"Nice to meet you, too," Owen's dad said with a smile.

"Sorry, I'm Johnny. I didn't meant to be rude. I'm a bit excited to crush Perry," I told him.

"No worries. We're looking forward to the same thing," he said, and I relaxed as he put the car into reverse and backed out of the driveway. At least, he began to back out of the driveway, but then he suddenly put on the brakes.

"Your mom," he said, and pointed to the upstairs window. Sure enough, she was leaning out of it, her hand shielding her eyes from the sun. He put the van back into park, and it seemed as if he was going to get out. My heart quickened and I saw my future as a pitcher slipping away.

"She's just saying good-bye," I said, and rolled down the window enough to stick my arm out, but not enough that she could see that my hair was pulled up and I didn't look like her daughter.

"Bye, Mom! Love you! See you tonight!" I called,

and hoped that was enough to keep her inside.

"Maybe I should talk to her?" Owen's dad asked. "Introduce myself?"

"Nope, we're good. She's putting my little sister down for a nap. You can meet her at one of our next games," I said, even though that would never happen.

He seemed to be debating what to do. I saw him glance from the window to the road a few times, and I said a silent prayer that he wouldn't decide to get out of the van.

Owen spoke up. "Let's get a move on."

"All right, game time it is," Owen's dad said, and I couldn't agree more.

He reversed out of the driveway, and I was never so happy to see Grandma's house disappear as we drove away. But while I was glad to have a ride to the game, there was no way I was getting picked up here ever again. I'd rather ride my bike all the way to an away game than chance another meeting between Mom and Owen's dad. Whether or not they thought it was odd, I vowed to make sure that I was always at Owen's house before they even got in the van, so they never came near Grandma's house again. Gabby, Johnny, and Owen's dad couldn't mix, and I needed to make sure to keep it that way.

EACH SUMMER DAY MOVED INTO THE NEXT, AND AS
time passed I could say with confidence that life was
good. Mom and Grandma still waited to watch me play
in the championship, I was able to convince Owen that
it was best for me to come to his house for rides to the
away games, and Dad and I e-mailed a few times a week
about the team. I was playing baseball, pitching in the
games, and loving it.

Today, before our game, I slipped into the bathroom
like I always did and ducked into one of the stalls. It was
another hot day, and I'd finished all the water in my water
bottle on the ride over. In other words, I needed to go to
the bathroom ASAP.

I was about to flush the toilet when I heard the door open. I peeked through the crack and saw three small girls begin to wash their hands at the sink. *No problem,* I thought, and worked on slicking my hair back and hiding it under my hat.

I waited in the stall until I heard the girls' chatter stop and the bathroom door close. I stepped out of the stall transformed into Johnny.

Right in front of two of the girls.

The smaller one screamed.

"There's a boy in the bathroom!" the other girl shouted.

"Sorry, sorry, sorry." I backed up toward the door as quickly as possible. I prayed their parents weren't outside and about to come racing in to find out what was wrong. "I must have gotten the men's room and women's room mixed up. I'm out of here."

And I was. I raced across the field to my team. I couldn't believe I was so stupid as not to check to make sure everyone had left. That could have ended a lot worse.

I stopped near home plate and bent over to catch my breath. The stands were full of families ready to watch our game, and I hoped those girls weren't at the park for the same reason.

YOU THROW LIKE A GIRL

"Johnny," Coach Marshall yelled. "You're pitching today. Start warming up."

"Got it." I tossed my bag near the bench and ran to left field, where Owen stretched.

"Are you ready to show this team that they can't mess with us?" Owen asked.

"I'm not giving them any mercy," I told him, and true to my word, we destroyed the opposing team. Our team played great. I struck out five players, Owen only let one person score, tagging out two others as they tried to cross home plate, and we beat the other team by seven runs. It was our sixth straight win of the season, and as the parents were saying, our team was on fire.

"Keep this up," Coach Marshall told us as we gathered around him after the game, "and we have a good chance of playing in the championship game at the Corn Festival."

And I'll be there pitching our way to a win, I thought.

William, our shortstop, came up to me as we all congratulated each other. "My parents said the team could come over for pizza. Do you want to hang?"

Usually I wouldn't say yes to an invitation like this, because while I felt confident I could fool everyone on the field, I wasn't so sure of how I'd be when I was outside my element. But today had rocked. I wanted to celebrate with the team, and pizza sounded awesome right now.

"You should come, Johnny," Owen said. "William's house is pretty sweet. He has a projector in his basement, so when we watch movies, they take up the whole wall."

"Okay, sure," I said. What harm could happen when you ate pizza and watched a movie, right?

Wrong.

I called my mom and told her I was going to a teammate's house for pizza. I just didn't tell her that my teammate was male. I got a ride with Owen's parents and soon found myself in William's basement with fourteen loud boys all trying to one-up each other by doing stupid things.

From my time on the team, I'd learned there was a specific language among boys, and it consisted of farts, burps, and spitting. While I'd never fart in front of the boys, I could burp louder than about half of them. It was a charming talent Dad had taught me when I was young. He thought it would be hilarious to have a three-year-old who could burp on command. What he didn't bargain for was that I'd be so good at it, and while Mom hated my burping and called it unladylike, Dad always cheered me on after I drank a can of soda and let out a giant belch. I figured I might as well use my talent to my advantage to fit in with the team.

William passed out cans of cherry soda, and Calvin took a long swallow from his and let a giant burp rip. Everyone cracked up. He patted his stomach with a proud look on his face.

"Not bad," I said, and all eyes turned to me. "But nothing compares to this beauty." From deep within me came a rumbling and a sound that left the team with their mouths hanging open.

Yes, ladies and gentleman, I'd shocked a roomful of boys with my monstrous burp. Baseball wasn't the only thing I could do better than them. I couldn't imagine what they would think if they found out I was a girl. And what Mom would say if she caught me acting like this. I laughed to myself as I imagined suggesting that perhaps instead of the dance I was trying to learn, I could use burping as my talent for the pageant. She'd probably pass out from mortification.

My victory was short lived, though, as the boys turned their attention to the giant projector Owen had mentioned. William turned on some video game that involved shooting zombies as they jumped out from behind rocks and trees and other dark places.

I sat back and watched as the boys competed with each other in this game they all knew how to play.

"What's the highest level you've gotten to on *Zombie Raid*?" asked Matthew, who sat next to me and was drinking his third soda.

I couldn't tell him I'd never played the game, when he automatically assumed not only that I had, but that I was skilled enough to make it past different levels. Did most boys play video games? From the looks of things in this basement, that seemed to be the case, so I wasn't about to reveal that I'd never even picked up a controller.

"A few weeks ago I almost made it to the end," I told him. I wasn't sure what the end was, but it sounded better than taking a guess at how many levels the game had.

"Really? Were you able to defeat the zombies in the graveyard level?"

"Oh, yeah, I've made it past that a number of times."

Matthew's eyes became huge, and he looked at me as if I'd told him Babe Ruth was my great-great-grandfather. "Whoa, I've never even been able to get that far, let alone defeat it. I've always wondered what it was like. People say that it's crazy, with zombies jumping out from behind tombstones."

Shoot.

Wrong answer.

The game was about zombies, so wouldn't the grave-yard level be an easy one? Isn't that where zombies come from? Apparently not, and now Matthew thought I was some hard-core gamer.

"Hey, everyone. Johnny's been able to get past the graveyard zone," he said to the group gathered on the couch. A few of the boys began to ask questions about how to beat different levels, and a controller was pushed into my hands.

Wait. No way. What had I gotten myself into? It was one thing to talk like I knew what I was doing, but it was a whole different thing to have to prove it to people.

"Can you teach me how to defeat the zombies in the jungle setting? I've never been able to get past that point," Matthew said.

"Um, yeah, sure. I can try," I said, because what else could I do? I wasn't about to admit to them that I hadn't been telling the truth.

So with everyone crowded around me, I proceeded to

start the game, and was killed immediately by a zombie.

"Ha, I'm a little rusty," I joked. "I haven't played this game in ages."

"But you said you almost made it to the end a few weeks ago," Matthew said.

"Yeah, that feels like ages ago, since I've been so busy with baseball," I quickly replied.

The game started again, and this time I was able to stay alive for over a minute, but mainly because I couldn't figure out how to use the controller, so my character stood in one place. A minute is how long it took for a zombie to come and get me.

"Are you sure you've made it to the end of this game?" Matthew asked, and gave me a suspicious look.

"Of course," I told him. "The problem is that this controller is completely different from my own; it's confusing."

"What's confusing about it? The red button is for walking and the blue is for jumping. The knob lets you move in different directions," Matthew said, and I silently cursed him for making me look like an idiot in front of everyone.

The game started for a third time, and right as my character began to move after I pressed the stupid red button, the door to the basement opened and William's mom yelled down to us.

"Pizza is here! Who wants to help me carry it?"

The boys around me scrambled to get up, and a few ran to grab the food while others grabbed plates and napkins, the game forgotten. I let out a giant breath, relieved that pizza trumped watching me make a fool of myself. I dropped my controller onto the floor and kicked it under the couch. Maybe they'd think it went missing and stop playing the game.

I walked to the table, where everyone was busy devouring the food. I couldn't believe I'd been such an idiot to lie about something like that. I waited for one of the boys to bring it up, but everyone was too busy stuffing their faces. I watched the game still playing on the projection screen. A zombie come out from behind a tree and killed my character again. I grabbed a piece of pepperoni and took a giant bite. Thank goodness for pizza.

THANKFULLY, MY AWFUL VIDEO-GAME-PLAYING SKILLS
were forgotten by our next game and the only thing I had
to be good at was pitching. And that was something I
didn't have to pretend I could do. I struck out five batters, and we won by six runs. I rode my bike home in the
best mood ever and was still smiling when I walked into
the house.

"There you are," Mom said. She was on the floor and
helped Ava stack some blocks on top of one another. Ava's
hair was in two tiny pigtails with bows wrapped around
them, and Mom had on another one of her sundresses. "I
was about to go to the ballpark and get you."

"What? Why would you do that?" I asked in a panic.

Mom couldn't come to the ballpark to get me. Ever.

"It's your dad—" she started.

"Is everything all right? Is he okay?"

"He's fine," Mom said quickly. "In fact, he's supposed to be calling in half an hour. I was worried you weren't going to make it home in time."

"He is?" I asked.

"Yep, pretty soon, so why don't you go clean up and meet us back down here."

She didn't have to tell me twice. I showered and changed in less than ten minutes, and slid into my seat at the kitchen table, ready to tell Dad about how Coach Marshall gave me the pitching position.

Except Dad didn't call at six p.m. like he had said he would.

And he didn't call at seven or seven thirty, either.

Two hours had passed with no Dad, when Mom finally spoke up.

"It looks like we won't be talking to him tonight," Mom said, and she sounded so sad. And not sad because you finished your cupcake or it's raining when you're supposed to go to the zoo sad, but sad like the day we dropped Dad off. That afternoon she'd been in her bedroom, and

I'd come to ask her a question, but when I'd seen her sitting on their bed looking at her wedding picture, I'd backed out, not wanting to bother her.

"Remember he was late last time," I said to help calm myself and everyone else.

"You're right." Mom gave me a weak smile, but two hours was beyond late. And when he still hadn't called after three hours, we had to admit that we weren't going to hear from him, which gave me a shaky feeling in my stomach. Dad had said he'd call, and if he didn't, what did that mean?

"I don't think he's calling," Mom admitted, and this time none of us argued or tried to come up with an excuse.

"Why didn't he call?" I asked, which was my way of asking if he was okay.

"I have no idea," Mom said. "But I'm sure he had a good reason."

"He probably had work to do that he couldn't get away from," Grandma added to make me feel better.

"Yeah, I bet he was busy," Mom said, but it didn't sound convincing. She turned to Ava, who had fallen asleep in her high chair. "I better get this tired little girl off to bed. I'm sure we'll hear from him tomorrow."

Ava whined and rubbed her eyes. It was way past her bedtime, and there was no reason for her to stay up now. Mom carried her out of the room, and Grandma walked to the cupboard.

"How about I make us some hot chocolate," she suggested and held up two mugs. "I have whipped cream that I can add to the top of it. I'll even let you put on as much as you want."

"I don't feel like it," I told her. "I'm going to bed."

"Of course, honey," she said.

I headed toward the stairs, but before I could go up them, she came over and wrapped her arms around me.

"Don't worry," she whispered. "Your dad is okay."

I nodded, because I was afraid that if I spoke, she'd be able to tell how worried I was, and I needed to stay strong for Mom. But as I headed to my room, I wondered how she could be so sure he was okay.

22

I SAT ON MY BED AND STREAMED THE END OF THE
Cleveland Indians game on my computer, because sleep
was the last thing I could do tonight. I opened my win-
dows to let in the breeze. The locusts had started their
evening song, and kids yelled as they played a late-night
game of tag somewhere close by. The familiar sounds of
summer should have put me in a good mood, especially
since the Indians were up by seven runs, but it wasn't
enough to take my mind off all my worries about Dad.
Something had to be wrong. Dad wouldn't ignore us.

I watched the ceiling fan above my bed spin around,
and my head did the same with thoughts about Dad.

What if he couldn't call us? How long would the military take to tell a family about something really bad?

The floor creaked outside my door, and I turned to find Mom standing there.

"Can't sleep either?" she asked. She had a glass of milk in her hand, and I knew it was warm. She always drank that when she was up too late. She claimed it was magic and helped her go back to bed.

"I wish I could."

Mom sat at the end of my bed and gestured to the computer. "Who's winning?"

"We are. We're so far ahead, they'll never be able to catch up."

The two of us watched the game quietly for a few minutes. I wished Dad was here cheering along with me and yelling at the bad calls the umps made. It didn't feel like summer without him. I missed him more than anything else in the world.

"Do you think Dad is okay?" I asked Mom, unable to not talk about it anymore. "I mean, he didn't call, and that can't be a good thing. He wouldn't make us worry, so maybe something is wrong." My voice broke on the word "wrong," and I hated that I couldn't be strong for Mom.

"He's fine. We'll hear from him," Mom said, her automatic reply. He could be suspended above a volcano about to erupt and she'd tell me all was good. That was the way it went.

23

DAD STILL HADN'T CALLED BY THE NEXT MORNING.
Mom tried to stay in a good mood, but she didn't fool anyone. She constantly checked her phone, and twice she walked to Grandma's computer to make sure it was still on. After breakfast was done, no one made a move to leave, and we all sat around the living room waiting for the same thing, even if we didn't want to admit it to each other.

Lunchtime came and went, and still nothing. Finally Mom stood and stretched.

"This is silly; we're wasting the whole day. We need to go out and do something to take our minds off everything."

Grandma changed Ava's diaper and dangled a rattle over her. "How about the two of you go out, and I'll stay here with this cutie." She tickled Ava on the stomach, and my sister giggled and clapped her hands.

"What a great idea! Gabby and I can go look for pageant dresses. I'm sure everything is picked over here, so how about we drive to Beachwood Mall? Dress shopping is always fun, right?" Mom asked hopefully.

"Sure, that would be great," I said, because I didn't want to disappoint her. However, shopping for a dress was the last thing I wanted to do, especially at Beachwood Mall, which was about an hour away and was where rich people who carried thousand-dollar purses shopped. But it was better than sitting around the house all afternoon thinking about what could have happened to Dad.

Mom grabbed her car keys, and a little over an hour later, the two of us were smack-dab in the middle of the department store's teen formal wear section. Upbeat music blasted through the speakers, and dresses of all colors and fabrics surrounded me. Mom was in love with every one of them, and if there was anything that would make Mom feel better, it was shopping for fancy dresses.

"Oh goodness, this is gorgeous!" She held up a shiny

blue dress that looked more like a raincoat. I scrunched my nose in distaste, and Mom sighed and put it back.

"How about this one?" She held up a short bright red dress.

"You're kidding, right? This is the Miss Popcorn pageant, not the Miss Tomato pageant."

"You can't disagree about every dress I pull out," Mom said. "You have to like something."

"You have to find something I like."

"I'm trying, but you're being difficult," she said, and okay, maybe she was right. I should probably have been more open-minded. After all, I was supposed to be playing along and making her feel better.

"How about you just pull some for me, and I'll try them on. I'll go sit over on the bench while you look."

"That's no fun," Mom said, and pouted. "Don't you want to help?"

"I trust you," I told her. "Find me something that's going to win the pageant."

Her face lit up, and she headed back into the racks of dresses to help fulfill her dreams of me winning the pageant. I sat and tried to think of anything but Dad, which was impossible. The Indians played today, and if

Dad had been here, we'd have been at home sitting on our porch streaming the game on his phone and cracking open peanuts, tossing the shells onto the ground. Mom always got mad and made us sweep them up, but we didn't mind. Throwing them down made us feel like we were at the game.

"All right, we're good," Mom said, interrupting my thoughts. "I've got a few dresses for you to begin with."

"A few" was putting it mildly. She must have had at least ten dresses in her hands, maybe more. They were stacked so high, I wasn't sure how she'd even made it over here without dropping a bunch.

"We're going to be here all week if I try every one of these on."

"There aren't that many," she said.

"Let's go." I stood up and headed toward the fitting room. "I better start right away, since the mall closes in five hours."

"Ha-ha," she said, but she cracked a genuine smile, which meant this trip had helped.

Mom might have been feeling better, but after I tried on my fifth dress, a horrific blue sparkly thing, I couldn't say the same about me.

"This is awful. These are all awful. Nothing looks good on me." I reached behind and tried to unzip the offending dress. I wanted it off and out of my sight. Everything I tried on made me look funny—too skinny, too lumpy, too fancy, too casual, too old, too young, too something. I felt like Goldilocks in a bad version of *Goldilocks and the Three Bears*.

"We simply haven't found the right one yet," Mom said, but I could tell she was frustrated too.

"Face it, I'm not a formal-dress kind of girl. These all look silly on me," I said, near tears.

"What about this one?" Mom held up an emerald-green dress made of a soft lightweight fabric. "The color is gorgeous."

She was right. The color was pretty, and I liked how the skirt was a bit longer than some of the other dresses.

"I'll give it a shot."

I headed back into the fitting room for yet another wardrobe change. I pulled off the blue monstrosity and threw it on top of the giant pile of discarded dresses. Other people around me talked and joked as they tried on clothes, and I wondered what was wrong with me that nothing worked. These dresses didn't feel right, and at this point I was afraid nothing would. But Mom had made it her mission to find me a dress today, and I didn't want to disappoint her.

Maybe this one will work, I thought as I shimmied into the green fabric. I zipped it up and slowly looked in the mirror, expecting to see another awful dress, but I didn't. Instead I looked kind of cute. It had thin straps and flared at the hips but wasn't too poufy.

Mom talked to someone outside the fitting room about the pageant. I swear, she could go anywhere and find someone to talk with about her favorite topic.

"What about this dress?" I asked as I opened the fitting room door. I stepped out and saw Mom with an older woman with dark hair done up perfectly in a bun and wearing a pearl necklace and earrings.

"Gabby, this is Mrs. Carpenter. She's here with her daughter looking for a pageant dress too. Isn't that fun?"

Mrs. Carpenter gave me a little wave with only her fingers, and the rings she had on sparkled under the lights. "Yes, we don't have a lot of time, do we? Pretty soon the only thing left to wear will be potato sacks." She laughed in this these short loud bursts, and I nodded to be polite, but she sounded like a cackling bird to me. She placed her hand on Mom's shoulder. "But I bet you'd still win even if you had to wear a potato sack. You always looked good in whatever you wore onstage."

"I doubt that," Mom said, but it probably was the truth.

I smoothed the sides of the dress with my hands. "Well, what do you think?"

Mom made a sad face. "Oh, boo, that one doesn't work either, does it?"

"Yeah, honey, green doesn't seem to be your color," Mrs. Carpenter chimed in, as if I even wanted her opinion.

All my good feelings whooshed out of me like the air from a balloon. I'd found a dress I liked, and both of them hated it. I tried hard to hold back tears, because I felt like a complete failure. I thought people put dresses on to look pretty and feel good about themselves, and here I felt the exact opposite.

"Now, there's someone who looks good in green," Mrs. Carpenter said as the door to the fitting room across from me opened and a girl stepped out in the exact same dress I had on.

Correction.

Jessa stepped out in the exact same dress I had on.

Of all the bad luck in the world, I had to get the worst

of it. What had I done to anger fate enough to place Jessa in the exact same fitting room as me in the dress Mom had just said didn't work for me? And everything about Jessa was perfection. Her hair was pulled back in a twist, and she had on a tiny bit of eye shadow and shimmery lipstick. I thought about the dirt under my fingernails and tried to remember if I'd put on deodorant today.

"You look stunning in that dress," Mom said, as if things weren't bad enough. "The color brings out the blue in your eyes."

Traitor, I thought, and shot invisible daggers with *my* eyes at Mom.

"Thanks," Jessa said in a voice dripping with fake sweetness. "I like it too, but then again, I like all the dresses I've tried on. How can I pick just one?"

She smiled at me, her lips a bright red. How could she keep her lipstick looking so good? When Mom would practice with my pageant makeup, I'd get the lipstick on my teeth. It got so bad that Mom decided that I'd only wear a little clear gloss, to avoid "any embarrassing slips," as she so nicely put it. Basically, she didn't think I could handle lipstick.

"We're still searching for the perfect dress," Mom

said, since Jessa and I obviously didn't have the same problem.

"Too bad," Jessa said. "But keep trying. I'm sure there has to be something that looks good on you."

"I keep telling her the same thing. We'll find one. We just need to do a bit more looking," Mom said, too oblivious to realize that what Jessa had said was a put-down and not some kind of encouragement.

"Yeah, well, I need to change so we can keep looking for the *perfect* dress," I told them, not even caring how rude I was. I raced back into the fitting room and leaned against the door. This was awful. There was not one fun thing about the pageant, and I was pretty sure it would drive me crazy sometime soon.

I yanked off the green dress as if it were on fire; I couldn't get out of it fast enough. I kicked it into the corner with all the other ugly dresses, wishing they would disappear. I didn't want to go back out there to face Jessa and her perfect dresses that all fit as if the designer had made them for her.

"We should buy both of these, and I can decide which one I want to wear," I heard Jessa say louder than she had to.

"That's a wonderful idea," her mom said. "You were

beautiful in each of them. Maybe we won't tell your father and you can keep both of them."

"I like the way you think," Jessa said, and I wanted to scream.

There was a knock on my fitting room door, but they had another thing coming if they thought I'd open it and face everyone again.

"Still changing," I said.

"Bye, Gabby," Jessa said. "Good luck finding the perfect dress."

I gritted my teeth and fought the urge to say something back at her.

I pulled on my shorts and T-shirt and stared at myself in the mirror. Why did this have to be so difficult? Why couldn't Mom see that I wasn't cut out to be Miss Popcorn?

"Good riddance," I said to the pile of dresses before I stepped out of the fitting room.

"I'm done for today," I told Mom in a tone that meant there was no room for arguing.

She got the message and didn't even try to change my mind. And the two of us walked out through the formal wear section full of rack after rack of dresses that did nothing but remind me of who I wasn't.

MOM AND I HARDLY TALKED ON THE CAR RIDE BACK.
We both had too much on our minds, so we were lost in
our own thoughts instead of combining our worries and
making them worse. The only time we said anything was
when Mom went through the drive-through to get dinner.

We found Grandma and Ava sitting in the big armchair
when we arrived home. Ava was asleep, and Grandma
had a book in her lap. Mom carefully picked Ava up and
said good night to us.

"Time to get this little girl off to bed," she said.

"How did it go today? Did you find a dress to wow
all the judges?" Grandma asked after Mom had left
the room.

I held up my hands to show her I had nothing. "It was awful. There wasn't one dress that looked good on me, and believe me, Mom had me try on every single one of them."

"I'm sure you'll find your dress. It's only a matter of looking a bit more."

"I doubt it. Nothing was remotely right in Mom's eyes. It was like each dress was a constant reminder that I wasn't cut out to do this."

The whole awful day came back to me, especially the part where Mom hated the only dress I liked. The one she thought looked great on Jessa.

"The pageant makes her happy, but there's only so much more of this I can take," I told Grandma, and as I said the words out loud, I realized it was the truth. "Mom isn't listening to me about what I want to do and what I want to wear. She tells me how to walk, what to say, what to wear, what my talent is. This isn't me competing; it's her competing through me."

"Your mom can get a bit carried away at times," Grandma said. "But she doesn't have bad intentions. Quite the opposite; she wants to help you."

"But she's changing me into someone I'm not. So why

even bother doing the pageant when I've become some cookie-cutter version of Mom?"

"What if you weren't like your mom? What if you did something different? Let's talk about the dress again."

I wrinkled my nose and fought the urge to shudder. "I'd rather not."

"Hear me out," Grandma said. "If you could have your dream dress, what would it look like?"

"Any kind of dress?"

"Any kind. Forget about what your mom wants. What do *you* want?"

I thought for a moment, trying to picture exactly what I had in my mind. "The dress would be short but not too short; it would end right below my knees. The skirt would flare out a little bit, but it wouldn't be crazy poufy like all those dresses Mom used to wear. It would have a sash around the middle, and I'd wear Converse sneakers with it."

"Oh yes, footwear is important. The sneakers are a must," Grandma agreed, and I loved her for it. "Now what about the color?"

I chewed on my bottom lip, trying to figure out the right color. I thought about the sky above me on a clear day when I stood on the pitcher's mound. "Blue. Bright blue like the perfect summer day."

"I can do that," Grandma said with a glimmer in her eye.

"Do what?" I asked, confused.

"Make your dream dress. Where do you think your mother got all her dresses?"

"You made them?" I asked. Why did I never know that?

"Every single one of them. Even the ugly poufy one. But I did it because that was her vision of a dream dress," Grandma said. "And now I'd like to make your dream dress."

"I'd love that!" I threw my arms around her. My mood was suddenly drastically better. "Yes, yes, yes!"

"I thought that might be the solution. We'll go to the fabric store tomorrow and find the color blue you have in mind, and I'll get started on it right away."

"I can't wait," I told her, and it was the truth. For the first time I was excited about the pageant and my dress because it would be exactly what I wanted and only what I wanted.

I HAD A DREAM THAT THERE WAS AN EARTHQUAKE AT
Grandma's house. Everything shook, and I needed to take cover. I got tangled up in my sheets and woke myself up, except the shaking didn't stop. I sat up, terrified.

"Gabby, honey, it's me," a soft voice said.

I froze, and as my eyes adjusted to the dark room, I could see Mom next to my bed.

"What time is it?" I asked, and peeked out the window. It was way too early to go jogging. The streetlights were still on, and I could see a sliver of moon above the trees.

"It's four thirty. Sorry to wake you, but it's important."

My mind flashed back to the call from Dad that we didn't get. "Is everything okay? Is Dad okay?"

"Yeah, honey, he's fine. In fact, he's on the computer right now if you want to go downstairs and talk to him."

"Now?"

"Yep, and I thought you wouldn't mind if I interrupted your beauty sleep, since I'm sure you want to talk to him."

"Do I ever!" I threw my covers off and jumped out of bed.

I ran down the steps so fast, I'm surprised I didn't slip and fall. I flew into the seat in front of the computer, and Dad looked at me from the screen, startled.

"Whoa there, Curveball. You couldn't even comb your hair for your dear old dad?" he joked.

I saw my image in the little box on the computer and had to laugh. My hair stuck up all over the place, giving the true meaning to the term "bed head."

"What are you talking about? This is the latest style. See what happens when you're gone too long?"

"I'm just glad I don't have to smell your morning breath," Dad joked, and pretended to fan his face. "That can be some horrible fumes."

"I see being overseas hasn't changed you," I told him.

"Not one bit. What about you? How are you doing? I'm sorry I couldn't call earlier; we were doing some field training and didn't make it back to the base in time."

"It's okay," I told him, even though it hadn't been, but I needed Dad to believe I could be strong for Mom.

"How's softball going?" he asked.

"Amazing," I told him, glad to have something to say that would make him happy. "Coach Marshall chose me to be the starting pitcher for the team. I pitch every game and strike people out left and right."

"That's wonderful!" He held his hand up to the screen for a virtual high five. "I bet those girls are still in a daze after coming up against the amazing new pitcher."

"Something like that," I told him. What would he think if he found out that I wasn't striking out girls but boys? Would he be proud of me, or mad that I was fooling everyone? Dad was all about winning, but he always told me you had to have good sportsmanship and play fair. Was what I was doing fair? I wasn't sure, because it also didn't seem fair that there wasn't a girls' team. I was only finding a way to play ball.

"When I was your age, I was the relief pitcher, so it sounds as if you're doing something right."

"I'm trying," I said. "And I've learned it all from you."

"Well, I'm glad you're having a good time. I hate that

I can't see you play, but remember I'm thinking about you every moment of the day. Twenty-four/seven."

"Every moment? Mom and Ava aren't going to be happy that you've forgotten about them," I joked.

"Okay, how about, I'm thinking of all three of you every moment of the day?"

"Sounds good," I told him, and wished I could talk to him 24/7. It felt so much better when I could see his face and didn't have to worry about whether he was okay.

We talked for about five more minutes, until it was time to end the call. "I miss and love you like crazy and can't wait to hear more about how you're striking out the entire town."

"I love you too, Dad," I said, and wished I could jump into the screen and be there with him.

Mom magically appeared behind me, and the two of us waved good-bye, neither of us wanting to end the call, so we waited until Dad signed off.

"Thanks for waking me," I told Mom.

"Of course. I figured if anything could drag you out of bed, Dad could."

"I'm glad he's okay," I said. It was just the two of us, so maybe we could talk about him being away.

"Me too," Mom said, and headed into the kitchen. "What do you think? Is it too early for a smoothie?"

I sighed and wished for once that Mom would open up and talk about Dad, because it was getting harder and harder to hold everything inside and continue to pretend for her that everything was all right.

THE MORNING TURNED INTO ONE OF THOSE DAYS
where the sky threatened to pour at any moment. Gray
clouds loomed, and a hot heavy breeze made it feel as
if you were living in an oven. It was prime weather for
a thunderstorm. I thought for sure our game would be
canceled, but when it still hadn't rained by midafternoon,
I jumped onto my bike and rode to the field. I made sure
to adjust the back of my hat a little tighter, so the wind
wouldn't blow it off. You could never be too careful.

I should have known the dark skies were a bad omen,
but I was too busy remembering how good it felt to talk
to Dad and how we were playing the only other undefeated team in the league. The Corn Festival would be

here before we knew it, and if we kept playing the way we were, a spot in the championship game would be ours for sure.

Coach Marshall called us all into a circle before the start of the game.

"All right," he said. "This is a big one. Take a look at all the people who are here to see us win and give Stuart Village their first loss."

We glanced at the stands, and he was right. They were packed for the game, even with the danger of rain. I spotted the familiar faces of my teammates' parents and siblings. Owen's dad was there with Owen's little brother, and AJ's twin sisters held up a sign they had made for him. I saw a few grandparents and even a German shepherd on a leash. It was as if the whole town had showed up to watch this game.

"You all can win today; don't believe for a second that you can't," Coach Marshall went on. He checked his clipboard. "The batting lineup goes AJ, Ben, Georgie, Johnny, Brian, Calvin, Sean, Jack, and Owen. I want to see all of you cross home plate this inning, okay?"

"Only once?" Sean joked, and we all agreed that once wasn't enough.

We gathered in around each other and placed our hands in the middle to say the chant we started each game with.

"Good, better, best. Never let it rest, until your good is better and your better is your best. Gooooooo, Chester!" We threw our hands into the air and cheered, before heading back to the bench. We were fired up and ready to go. AJ went to bat, and I did practice swings while I waited for my turn.

Pitching might have been my specialty, but I wasn't too shabby at hitting either. I'd never gotten a home run, but I usually made it onto base and have had a few doubles. So when I stepped up to the plate today, I felt pretty confident I'd make it on base.

I used my own trick when on the mound and stared down the pitcher, trying to play with his mind. I didn't break eye contact until he let go of the ball, and when he did, I was ready for it. The crack of my bat as it connected sent the crowd into a frenzy of cheers as AJ made it home and scored. I ran to first as fast as I could and made it there before the ball did. I'd helped bring in our first run, and my team was now in the lead. The next two batters helped continue my path around the bases, and

I soon found myself on third. We were ahead by three runs, and I planned to make it four.

"Woo-hoo, make it home, Johnny," one of the parents in the stands yelled.

I turned toward the voice, but I couldn't spot who had cheered for me. But what I did spot, up top on the opposite team's side, was Jessa.

If I'd been a cartoon character, my jaw would've dropped all the way to the ground. This had to be some kind of bad dream, because how was it possible to run into her two days in a row when I didn't want to see her at all?

I snuck another look because maybe it was only someone who looked like her.

Nope. There was no mistaking her. She was way too dressed up for a baseball game, in a skirt and tank top. I couldn't tell from where I was, but I would've bet money she had makeup on too. Jessa took this idea of being pageant-ready to a whole new level, showing up at a dusty baseball field looking as if she were going to prom.

She was deep in conversation with an older woman next to her, and I hope she hadn't already spotted me. I kept my face turned away from her, but I had to pitch again. I wouldn't be able to hide. What if Jessa recognized me as Gabby?

Before I could figure out what to do, there was a flurry of cheers.

"Run, Johnny, run!" a voice yelled, and I saw Brian speeding toward me from second base. I'd been so lost in my thoughts that I hadn't even realized the next batter had hit the ball. I raced to home plate, Brian right behind me, so close that I could hear him breathing hard. We crossed over the plate, one after the other, and although the people in the stands went crazy from the excitement, my team didn't look as happy.

"What the heck was that, Johnny? You were acting like some girl, daydreaming on base. You almost cost us two runs," Calvin said to me.

Oh no, please tell me he didn't. Did he really just say that?

I gave him my dirtiest look and took a deep breath to try to calm myself down a bit.

"Some girl? Excuse me? Acting like some girl?" I said, enraged. "I'd be careful what you say. I bet a lot of girls could kick your butt in baseball."

"Yeah, right," he said, and smirked. "And my grandma can outrun me in cross-country."

I was about to dish it right back to him in support of girls everywhere, but I didn't want to make a scene and call more attention to myself. I'd have to set Calvin straight another time. Right now I needed to get far away, and I needed to do it immediately.

I clutched my stomach and walked to where Coach Marshall stood.

"What happened out there?" he asked when he saw me, thankfully in a nicer way than Calvin.

"I'm sorry. I'm not feeling well." I hated what I was about to do; I wanted to play in this game more than anything else and help keep us undefeated, but drastic times called for drastic measures. "I thought I was going to get sick."

"Understandable. It is hot out there." He thrust a bottle of water at me. "Take a seat on the bench and drink this."

"No," I told him. "It won't help. My stomach is cramping, and I'm pretty sure I have a fever."

He paused for a moment, and I worried he could tell I was faking. But he nodded and gestured toward one of the parents who helped as our third-base coach. "Go tell Mr. Powers what's wrong. He can call your parents to come pick you up. I need to figure out who is going to pitch in your place."

I headed over to Mr. Powers, but I certainly didn't tell him to call Mom. Instead I waited until Coach Marshall was busy looking at his playbook. Then I veered back to the bench to grab my baseball gear. I figured I could let him believe I had called my parents, because what he didn't know wouldn't hurt him, right? Although, that sounded like the motto for my life lately, and I was beginning to hate it.

"I'm heading home," I told Owen. I made sure to keep my back to the stands so Jessa wouldn't have another chance to see my face. "I don't feel good. Do me a favor and make sure we win this game."

"Are you sure you can't play? The two of us are only awesome when we pitch and catch together. I need you," Owen said, and at that moment I was glad to have a teammate like him.

"You'll do great," I told him. "And when you get home, you can call me and tell me about how badly you all crushed the other team."

"I like the sound of that," Owen said.

"Yeah, well, don't bother calling unless you guys win," I joked.

Once Owen turned his attention back to the game, I snuck away. I couldn't risk staying a second longer with Jessa in the stands.

27

TRUE TO HIS WORD, OWEN CALLED AFTER THE GAME
yesterday to report that our team had in fact won. "We
destroyed them," he said, and while we still had a few
more teams to play, they'd all be easy to beat. And with
that win our spot in the championship was pretty much
guaranteed. I wrote Dad an e-mail telling him as much,
excited that I was so close to being able to fulfill my
promise to him.

But while baseball was great, that wasn't the case
with the Miss Popcorn pageant. Mom made some adjust-
ments to the dance for the talent portion to make it easier, but Ava could probably do it better than me. When
we practiced, Mom would tell me to be graceful, but it

was no use, I felt like a giant elephant trying to jump and twirl around.

It was as if, whatever I did, no matter how many times, I simply couldn't do it right. So I was glad when Mom suggested we take a day off and have a spa day.

"It'll be fun," she said. "You can invite Erin and we'll get pampered."

I'd never been to a spa before, and it did sound like a lot of fun. I agreed and soon found myself sitting with my hands dipped in hot wax while my feet soaked in a warm tub of water. Mom had set up manicures and pedicures for us while she had a massage. Erin and I sat in chairs next to each other with glasses of sparkling grape juice to sip. I might not have been into the pageant prep, but this was something I could get used to.

"Are you sure you don't want nail polish on your fin- gernails?" the manicurist asked.

"No, thanks. I like the natural look," I told her.

"Boring," Erin said. She had picked out a glittery aqua polish that reminded me of a mermaid, and while it would have been fun to try a color like that, it wouldn't exactly work to show up at baseball practice with my nails painted. Mom would be mad that I didn't get any polish on, but I had no idea how I'd be able to explain that one to Coach Marshall and the boys.

"My toenails will make up for it." I gestured at the bottle of lime-green polish I'd chosen. I could at least have some fun with my toes, since they'd be covered up.

"If you say so," Erin said, and took a sip of her grape juice.

I picked up the polish bottle and twirled it around in my hand. I loved the idea of my secret toenails. They would reflect my real life; on the outside I'd look like Johnny when I pitched, but hidden underneath would be a little touch of something girly!

AFTER WE CAME HOME FROM THE SPA, I RAN UPSTAIRS
and changed into my baseball uniform for our game.
It was safe to say I'd become a master at juggling my
two personas. My mornings were spent preparing for
the pageant, and in the afternoons I'd slip away and ride
my bike to the playing field.

Grandma stopped me before I left for baseball and
mentioned how busy my days were.

"It's like you have two different lives. In the morning you're Gabby the Pageant Girl and in the afternoon
you're Gabby the Athlete. The two aren't usually paired
side by side, but I love that you can be both."

"Just call me Clark Kent. I can change from a skirt

to a baseball uniform in no time. I fool everyone with my magical transformation," I joked, but little did she know that it was a bathroom and not a phone booth where my change happened.

I slipped out of the house and raced to the park. My transformation had to be quick, because I'd mixed up the game time and was already late.

The team was warming up when I arrived, and soon I was jogging around the bases with them. I searched the bleachers, praying Jessa wasn't there. I checked, double-checked, and then checked one more time, but thankfully there was no sign of her.

"How are you feeling?" Owen asked me, running up alongside me.

"Fine, why?" I asked.

Owen gave me a funny look. "Because two days ago you were about to puke your guts out on the field."

"Oh, yeah, right. I'm fine now. Whatever it was must have been a twenty-four-hour bug," I told him, although it was more like the Jessa bug.

"Good. We need you for these last three games. Zach was horrible at pitching. We almost lost the game because of how many hits he allowed."

"Don't worry. I'm not going anywhere," I told him. "And I made sure to drink lots of orange juice for vitamin C, so I should be in tip-top shape."

Owen wasn't the only one who asked me how I felt as we moved through warm-ups. A bunch of my teammates commented and told me how glad they were to have me back. It felt good to know everyone counted on me so much, and when I stood on the pitcher's mound at the start of the game, I made sure to give it my all so I wouldn't disappoint anyone.

The team we were playing was no match for us, but what they lacked in talent they made up for in tricky plays. They bunted, stole, and waited to be walked to get on base. We should've been able to beat them easily, but they changed their strategy so often, we never knew what was coming.

The score was tied when a giant dark-haired boy who looked like he should have been in high school stepped up to the plate. The last time he'd batted, he'd hit a ball deep into the outfield and made it to second base. Our team was prepared for him to do that again, and everyone stepped back a few feet in preparation.

I threw my first pitch, and it whizzed past him.

"Strike!" the umpire yelled.

Owen gave me a thumbs-up as the batter hit his bat against the ground a few times. He got back into position and scowled at me.

I let the ball go.

"Strike two!"

The crowd cheered, and I was ready to put this guy back on the bench. Owen signaled at me to throw a changeup, which usually made the batter pop the ball up into the air, so that it was an easy catch.

I drew my arm back and let the ball go. He swung and connected. I waited for the ball to fly over my head, but instead he drove it into the dirt.

The grounder came at me before I had time to react and cracked me right on the ankle. I fell down as pain raced up my leg. I clutched at the spot where the ball had hit and told myself not to cry because I needed to look tough. But even tough guys wouldn't have been able to handle this pain, and I swiped my tears away.

The two players on the other team ran the bases and scored before one of my teammates could grab the ball and stop them. The ump called a time-out, and soon I had a crowd around me.

"Can you walk on it?" Coach asked, and gestured to

my foot, which was covered in my lucky socks. So much for them helping me.

"I don't think so," I said, my voice shaky. "It hurts really bad."

"Back up, boys. Give Johnny room," Coach Marshall said. "I'm going to help you off the field. Lean against me, but don't put any weight on the foot."

He pointed at Owen. "Run to the concessions stand and tell them we need a bag of ice."

He led me to the bench, where I sat down. Coach gestured to my foot. "You're going to need to take off your shoe and sock, so we can ice it. We want to get any swelling and bruising down as quickly as possible."

I began to untie my shoe, but then stopped.

My pedicure.

I dropped my laces. I couldn't take off my sock; everyone would see my toes.

"I'm suddenly feeling better," I said. "I guess it wasn't as bad as I thought it was." I tried to stand up, but as soon as I put even a teeny bit of weight on my foot, I fell back down and gasped in pain.

"You're not going anywhere," Coach Marshall said, and grabbed the ice Owen had brought him. "Let's ice your ankle before it gets worse and you're not able to pitch in the Corn Festival."

"That might happen?" I asked, and just like that I pictured all my dreams of pitching during the championship vanish. I had no choice. I pulled off my shoe and sock, and there, in all their lime-green glory, were my newly polished toenails.

To Coach Marshall's credit, he didn't say a word. He simply placed the ice over my ankle and told me not to take it off.

Owen, on the other hand, gave me a funny look. I turned away from him and inspected the ground.

Coach Marshall pulled out his cell phone. "Go ahead and give your mom a call, so she can come pick you up. Make sure to tell her it isn't an emergency when she answers. I don't want her to worry."

She'd worry, all right, I thought. As soon as she showed up here and saw me dressed like a boy and playing on a baseball team, and learned that I'd lied to her, my ankle would be the least of my problems. I was not making that phone call.

"It's okay," I told Coach Marshall. "I can ride my bike home."

"You most certainly cannot," he said, and waved the phone at me. I took it grudgingly.

I tried again. "My little sister isn't feeling well, so I don't want to make my mom come here when she's sick."

"Call your mom. I'm not going to get an earful from her because I didn't notify her when you got hurt."

"She wouldn't do that—" I started, but he cut me off.

"Call her," he demanded.

Owen pointed at the phone. "Type in your number and I'll call," he offered.

Owen took a few steps away from us. I watched, wide-eyed, as he held the phone to his ear and then began to talk.

"Hi, Mrs. Ryan. This is Owen. Nothing is wrong, but Johnny was hit in the ankle by a baseball. . . . Yeah, he's fine, we've put ice on it, but it's hard for him to walk. . . . No, it's okay. My mom can give him a ride home. Don't worry about coming here. . . . Okay. . . . Yeah, great. . . . Thanks. Bye."

He handed the phone to Coach Marshall. "Johnny can get a ride home with me, so we're all good."

Coach Marshall nodded and shook his finger at me. "Now, I want you to make sure you keep icing your ankle for as long as you can and stay off it. If you rest, you should be okay to pitch in a few days, which is exactly when we need you."

"I'll do whatever it takes," I told him, and promised myself that I'd freeze my foot in a box of ice if I needed to. I would be pitching in a few days. I'd make sure of that.

I watched the rest of the game from the bench. When he wasn't catching, Owen purposely sat on the other end so I couldn't talk to him. He made me sit through the whole game wondering what was going on. There was no way he had called Mom. She'd have no idea who Johnny was, so why would he pretend to talk to her? What was he trying to do?

The game ended with another win, keeping us undefeated. Coach Marshall told me one more time to keep icing my ankle, and I promised I would. It was already feeling a bit better, but from the way my ankle was changing color, there was going to be a very nasty bruise.

Owen finally sat next to me as the rest of the team cleared out.

"Did you really call my mom?" I asked.

"I only pretended to call her," he said. Then he gestured toward my foot. "How's your ankle feeling, Gabby?"

"A little bit better. Coach Marshall thinks I'll still be

able to pitch," I said, and then gasped. I put my hand over my mouth.

"Just what I suspected," Owen said. "I kept trying to figure out why Erin's friend at the pool was so familiar, and when I saw your socks, I remembered her friend was a die-hard Indians fan, and with the painted nails, everything clicked."

"Please don't tell anyone," I begged him. Now that he'd discovered my secret, I was doomed.

Even if my ankle healed, I could now kiss my chance to pitch good-bye.

"Like how you didn't tell anyone who you really were?"

"I know it wasn't right, but I had to do it."

"That doesn't make sense. Why would you have to do something like that?"

"So I could play ball for the Chester rec center," I told him. "There isn't a girls' team because of the pageant. This was the only way."

"There isn't a girls' team?"

"Not enough people signed up, so if you wanted to play, you had to join Riverside's team."

"No way. I'd never play for them," Owen said, pretty much as outraged as I was when I heard the news.

"Exactly."

"That doesn't seem right. I couldn't imagine not having baseball."

"Me either. That's why I pretended to be Johnny."

"I get that, but it doesn't make it okay. I also can't imagine not counting on my pitcher when I'm catching. I thought we had a good thing going. We're supposed to trust each other, but this whole time you lied to me."

"I didn't want to lie to you, but I was afraid if anyone found out, I'd get kicked off the team."

"You're good, Gabby. Your being a girl doesn't make a difference to me."

"But it will to other people." I thought back to what Calvin had said about girls playing ball. He was a perfect example of why I didn't want anyone to know about who I really was. "Please don't say anything. I have to pitch in the championship."

He must have heard the desperation in my voice, because he didn't ask any more questions.

"I won't say anything," he said, and if it wasn't for my hurt ankle, I probably would have jumped up and thrown my arms around him in thanks. "But that doesn't mean I'm cool with what you did. We have to be honest with each other."

"Deal," I told him. "No more secrets. Ever."

"Besides, I need you on the team. You're a great pitcher . . ."

"For a girl?" I finished, ready to battle again if I needed to about how girls were as good as boys.

"No, period. You're the best pitcher I've ever seen in summer league. You're crazy if you think I'm going to say anything to risk losing you. Although I'm not sure I can ever forgive the fact that you cheer for Cleveland," he said, a true Pittsburgh fan.

"I'll try not to remind you of how awesome my team is," I said.

"Hmmm, on second thought, maybe I'll say something to the team . . . ," Owen started.

"Wait! I take it back," I joked with him. "Pittsburgh is the best team around."

"Okay, then your secret is safe with me," Owen declared, and I felt like he'd told me I won the lottery.

I could still play!

Everything would be fine.

FOUR DAYS LATER MY ANKLE WAS STRONG ENOUGH
for me to pitch in our final regular-season game, a game
we won, which made it official. We were playing in the
Corn Festival championship! And I was the pitcher!

It had been a great day, and I was deep into a daydream
about the championship when I headed to the bathroom
to change after the game. Maybe it was because my mind
was somewhere else, but I took my hat off before I walked
into the bathroom.

Big mistake.

Because standing at the sink, putting on lip gloss,
was Jessa.

I froze, and the door swung back into me, giving me

a little push forward into the bathroom, the last place I wanted to be at the moment.

It took Jessa a few seconds to fit the pieces together, but when she did, she smiled as if she had been crowned Miss Universe.

"Well, I guess I should say congratulations," she said. "Looks like your team is going to be in the Corn Festival championship."

"You were at the game?" I said, and immediately wished I hadn't. I should've acted like I had no clue what she was talking about. Denied everything. Instead I was stupid enough to place myself at the scene of the crime.

"I was, which is why I'm so confused." She pointed at my uniform. "I just watched Chester win, but they played against my brother's team. My *brother*."

I tried to think of a way to fix my mistake and blurted out the first thing that came to mind. "We have the same-color uniforms."

"Yeah, no. There isn't a girls' team this year. My cousin had to join Riverside's team. So nice try, and I'm pretty sure pretending to be a boy is against the rules. And wouldn't it be a shame if your team got disqualified."

"Please, please, please don't tell," I said, and hated

that I had to beg Jessa for anything. But desperate times called for desperate measures, and this was most definitely one of those times.

Jessa shrugged. "I'll think about it. But right now I have to go back to my family. We're going out for pizza because my parents want to cheer up my brother. His baseball team lost the chance to play in the championship game. He's upset, because those *boys* were good."

And before I could try to explain, she walked out, leaving me all alone in my uniform. I stared at myself in the mirror.

"What have you done?" I asked my reflection. "The team has worked so hard. They counted on you, and now you might've ruined everything."

I didn't even bother to consider that maybe, just maybe, Jessa would keep her mouth shut. Because from what I'd already seen with Jessa, she'd never keep something like this to herself. It was only a matter of *when* she'd tell and what it would do to everyone who'd trusted Johnny.

GRANDMA WAS SITTING ON THE FRONT PORCH WHEN I
rode up on my bike.

"Well?" she asked.

"We won," I told her, and tried to muster a little excitement, but my mind kept flashing back to the look on Jessa's face when she figured out what I'd been doing.

"That's incredible! Does that mean we finally get to see you pitch?" Grandma asked, her face hopeful.

Shoot. That was the agreement, and I couldn't very well go back on it. There was no way Grandma and Mom would miss the championship game. But I guess at that point it wouldn't matter, since it would be the final game.

And besides, I probably wouldn't even be playing in it, if Jessa had her way.

"Yep, you'll finally get to see me pitch," I confirmed, and she clapped her hands together in happiness. An awful feeling filled my stomach. Grandma was looking forward to seeing me play, and I was sure Mom wanted to do the same. And I couldn't even think about Dad at the moment. I *had* to convince Jessa not to say anything. There was no doubt in my mind. This was too important.

"I can't wait," Grandma said. "And speaking of not being able to wait, I have a surprise for you hanging on the back of the door in my bedroom."

"You finished my dress?" I asked, with a mix of excitement and nervousness.

"I did, and I can't wait to see you in it. Go take a quick shower and then try it on!"

I took the fastest shower in the world and then ran to her room. I let out a squeal of joy, because it was the most beautiful dress in the world.

It was exactly how I'd imagined it, a blue that matched the sky outside my window. I picked the dress up, and the fabric was soft and cool in my hands. There were tiny sparkles all over it, and the bottom layer of the skirt was a pink ruffle fabric. I dried off with my towel and pulled the dress over my head. After adjusting the silver sash that tied around my middle, I gazed at myself in the mirror. It was better than I'd ever dreamed it would be. I loved the dress, every single part of it.

"You look beautiful," a voice said behind me. I turned, and Mom stood in the doorway.

"Do you think?" I turned back to my reflection. I thought about the awful shopping trip we'd had and how nothing had felt right. But this dress here, this felt right.

"Now it makes sense why all the other dresses didn't work. It was because this is the one for you."

"Grandma made it exactly how I described it to her. I can't even believe it's real." I couldn't help it; I turned around and twirled, loving how the skirt flared out a little.

"Now you're ready for the pageant," Mom said.

"Almost ready," I corrected her. "It still needs the finishing touch."

I ran to my room and dug around in the closet until I found my light purple Converse sneakers. I stuck my feet into them and walked back to Grandma's room.

I stood in front of Mom. "The perfect pair of matching shoes."

"I think . . . ," Mom slowly said, and I held my breath, nervous she'd say something about how they weren't pageant material, "there couldn't be a more perfect accessory for you."

They were. And I was going to wear them with the most gorgeous dress in the world.

THE NEXT FEW DAYS PASSED AND I DIDN'T HEAR FROM
Jessa. I tried to convince myself that was a good sign.
Maybe she wouldn't say anything, but that was about as
realistic as finding bigfoot in the woods or the pot of gold
at the end of the rainbow. In other words, impossible.

I figured I'd get my answer today, since it was the
run-through for the pageant, a practice session to make
sure we all knew what to do when it came time for the
real deal. The festival started this weekend, and there
was an excited hum in the air; the whole town couldn't
wait to welcome in the fiftieth anniversary of celebrat-
ing corn.

Mom dropped me off, and I was soon surrounded

by tulle, satin, silk, a mixture of perfumes, hair spray, lipsticks, double-sided tape, Vaseline, curling irons, and tons of other beauty products I didn't even recognize. Girls ran around screeching in shrill voices about missing tap shoes, and blisters on their feet from heels that hadn't been broken in.

"Okay, ladies. Make sure all of your stuff is in your station and then come take a seat," said Mrs. Sylvan, a woman who referred to herself as the "Head Miss Popcorn Coordinator." Never mind the fact that she was the *only* coordinator. She dressed as if she were going to some big-deal event, in a silk blouse, red skirt, pearls, and shiny black shoes. She wore a headset and barked orders into it to the high school students who volunteered as stagehands. When one of the girls mixed up and placed some cornstalks in the wrong place on the stage, Mrs. Sylvan yelled at the girl as if her life depended on making sure they were in the perfect spot. Truthfully, I was a bit afraid of her.

I put everything in the locker marked for me. The festival is always held in a giant field that's only used for the weeklong celebration. For the rest of the year it's empty, as if it's sacred ground that nothing else can happen on.

A stage is constructed every year for the pageant, seats are rented, and a tent is brought in as our dressing room. Some ancient lockers were donated by a local high school for us to store our stuff in.

Erin and I sat down where the audience would sit during the pageant and waited for everyone else to join us.

Just like I'd predicted, Mom had upped the practice time this past week, so if I wasn't at baseball, I was going over and over my dance or repeating all the pageant tips she'd given me. I was on summer vacation, but a lot of the time it felt as if I were back in school. Mom was happy, though, and it took both our minds off Dad, which was what mattered.

"Are you ready for this?" I asked Erin.

"I was born ready," she said as Jessa stepped out from behind the curtain onto the outdoor stage. Unlike the rest of us, who had entered from the side, Jessa walked right across to where Mrs. Sylvan stood. I had to admit she had the pageant walk down. Mom would probably have given one of her crowns away for me to be able to walk like Jessa. She whispered something into Mrs. Sylvan's ear, and Mrs. Sylvan stopped for a moment to laugh. The two of them were like old friends catching up with each other.

Jessa walked down the narrow steps without even faltering in her heels, and up the aisle. I slunk down in my seat and tried to make myself invisible, but it didn't work. When she made it to the two of us, she stopped. I could see the glitter in her eye shadow as she bent toward me.

"Wow, Gabby. I had no idea you'd clean up this well after you played on that dirty, dusty baseball field."

Before I could even think of a comeback, she whirled around and walked away, leaving me with a giant whiff of fruity perfume.

"What was that about?" Erin asked, as I secretly flipped out. This was it. I could kiss all my hard work good-bye.

"Oh, that. It's nothing. She saw me playing a pickup game of baseball the other day with some kids in my neighborhood. One of the boys asked her to join us, and she acted as if we were nuts," I said, adding another lie to the pile of lies I'd already told Erin. I hated it, but in a week the Corn Festival would be over, and I wouldn't have to hide who I was anymore.

"Typical Jessa," Erin said. "I bet the most athletic thing she's ever done in her life was run to the mall before it closed."

"Or turned every twenty minutes to get the perfect tan," I joked, so things would appear normal, but inside I was a nervous wreck about what Jessa knew.

Mrs. Sylvan began to talk to everyone, but I didn't hear a word she said. People say that before you die, your life flashes before you. Well, the same is true before a secret is revealed. My summer of playing baseball flashed through my mind. The strikeouts, base hits, crowds cheering, friendships, and most important, Dad's proud comments every time we talked or e-mailed. I saw it all, and my heart ached because I was going to lose it. Jessa had just made that clear, so now the situation was a ticking time bomb, and I was left to wonder when it would all explode.

PAGEANT PRACTICE COULDN'T GO FAST ENOUGH, AND I
bolted to Mom's car when it was over, but she jumped
out and told me she wanted to catch up with her friend
Cindy. Parents weren't allowed to watch the pageant
practice, but Mom said the rules didn't state that she
couldn't talk with the judges after practice, and now,
suddenly, Mrs. Sylvan was her long-lost friend and they
had to talk.

"Mom, that's embarrassing. What's everyone going to
say when they find you buttering up the judges?"

"I'm not buttering anyone up," she insisted. "I'm
talking to an old friend. Relax."

But relaxing was the last thing I could do after what

Jessa had said to me. I'd watched her during the whole rehearsal and waited for her to do something. I'm sure she enjoyed making me squirm, because she walked toward me two different times and then veered off in the other direction. Once she even winked as she walked away. My stomach was so full of nerves, it felt as if I'd swallowed an egg beater.

"What a surprise, your mom is bribing the judges," a voice said behind me.

Jessa stood there, still in her heels. How did she wear those things for so long?

"She's not bribing anyone. She's friends with Mrs. Sylvan," I said, using Mom's exact argument that only minutes ago I didn't believe.

"Sure, whatever you say," Jessa replied. "Because I should trust you, right? You're so truthful about things."

"Listen, I can explain," I told her.

She cut me off. "There's nothing to explain. It's just too bad you and Erin are dropping out of the pageant."

"We're what?" I asked, confused.

"Quitting the pageant. At least that's what you told me."

"I never ever said that."

"Yes, you did. Remember? We talked about it in the

bathroom the other day. Or do I need to remind you about our conversation?"

"No," I said quickly, and glanced toward Mom. Jessa could destroy everything right now if Mom heard her. I lowered my voice and pleaded with Jessa. "I can't do that. Erin's worked so hard for this, and my mom would be devastated."

"But you told me you would. You can't go back on your word. That wouldn't be *truthful*. And we both know how much you value honesty."

A car horn beeped from the parking lot, and I jumped, startled by the noise. Jessa's mom hung out of the window of the car.

"Jessa, get out of the sun this instant. You'll get tan lines that will look hideous onstage. How many times do I have to remind you?"

Jessa glanced at me quickly and then back to her mom.

"I was talking to Gabby," she said through gritted teeth.

"Oh, sorry. I didn't see you there," her mom called to me. "Jessa, love, we need to go. You have an upper-lip and eyebrow wax in ten minutes."

Jessa lowered her voice as she said her next words. "It's your call. I'll keep your secret safe if you want me to, but that means no pageant. For you or Erin."

She gave a little wave and headed toward her mom.

"What do you think you were doing?" her mom snapped when Jessa reached her. She must have thought I couldn't hear, because the next words out of her mouth were even meaner. "I thought I told you to stay away from Gabby. She's your competition, remember? Or is that too hard for you to understand, since you can't seem to get anything right these days?"

Jessa mumbled something I couldn't hear. Her mom pulled the car out of the parking lot, and they drove away. I stood motionless in my spot, an incredulous look on my face. I'm sure if someone had walked past, they'd have thought I'd gone crazy. But what was crazy was Jessa's mom. Did she actually believe I was competition? I wasn't a threat to them, especially since I couldn't even remember the right way to turn during my dance and had a very real fear of freezing up and not knowing what the heck to say during the interview portion. I had no idea why Jessa thought she needed to get me out of the pageant.

Erin, on the other hand, made perfect sense.

Erin was amazing and stood a chance of winning. Of course Jessa would want to get rid of her.

How could I ask Erin to drop out of the pageant? She was so excited about it and had worked so hard with Mom.

But what was the alternative?

Competing meant Jessa would ruin my chances of being able to play in the championship, and I needed to pitch in that game.

I ran my hand through my hair in frustration and wished I had a bat so I could take a few swings at the air.

I had no idea what I should do now that Jessa had thrown me this curveball.

THE NEXT MORNING I WAS STILL TRYING TO FIGURE out what to do about Jessa's threat. It was like I was in the middle of a tug-of-war. On one side was Dad, who was overseas serving our country. I'd promised him that I'd pitch in the championship game; I had given him my word. He was depending on me. But on the other side was Erin and Mom, who had both been working so hard to make sure we were ready for the pageant.

So what was I supposed to do? I had two different choices, and whichever I picked, someone would lose. There was no good solution and time was running out. Both the pageant and the championship game were days away.

I sent a message to Maddie, hoping she'd have a solution. There was nothing like hometown BFF love, and I needed a lot of that right now.

Worst ever. Johnny has been found out.

What? No!

: (: (: (: (: (: (

Can you still play ball?

Team doesn't know yet. But I'm sure they will soon.

Can you do anything???

Yeah. Quit pageant. I'm being blackmailed.

!!!!!!!!!

Don't know what to do.

Don't compete???

My mom would be sooooooo upset.

She would understand.

I know, but . . .

I sent the text unfinished, because she was right. Mom would understand, but she wasn't the only one involved. If I wanted to drop out of the pageant, Erin would also have to, and that wasn't fair.

Tell your mom. You need to play in that game!!!

Maddie was right. I did need to tell them. But it

wasn't really Mom I needed to tell. It was Erin.

I had to come clean to her.

It was time for her to meet Johnny. I just hoped that after she did, she'd still want to be friends with Gabby.

LIFE WAS ALWAYS BETTER WHEN ICE CREAM WAS
involved, and I needed as much "better" as I could get
right then. This called for an emergency meet-up at
Coneheads, which Erin immediately agreed to when I
texted her. Less than an hour later the two of us sat at a
picnic table under a tree and went to work devouring our
ice cream cones.

"So I need to tell you something," I told her as I tried
to keep the drips of mint chocolate chip from falling onto
my shirt. I could only imagine what Mom would say if
I came home covered in stains. She'd already warned
me that my appearance was very important these last
few days because "You never know who's watching." It

sounded like some messed-up version of Santa Claus knowing if I've been naughty or nice, but instead the magical pageant organizers would know if I was dressed like a lady or a slob.

"I'm all ears," Erin said. "What is this big mystery that was so major, you needed ice cream? Not that I need an excuse for ice cream."

"You might get mad at me," I told her, afraid to tell her the truth. We'd become good friends this summer, but I'd also been lying to her about the baseball team, and because of my lies, I'd dragged her into this mess.

"I can take it," she said. "I'm tough. How else would I be eating this cone so fast without getting an ice cream headache?"

I laughed. "True. But this is a bit more major." I took one last moment before I told her everything. "I've been keeping a secret from you and, well, basically everyone."

"I like secrets. Spill it," she said.

"The thing is, I've been playing baseball in the evenings."

"Baseball? With the other kids in your neighborhood?"

"No, on the rec center team."

"Wait, I'm confused. Riverside's team?" she asked.

"Chester's," I told her, and bit my lip. "I've been pulling back my hair, tucking it under a hat, and pretending to be a boy. I wasn't sure it would work, but it did. It was actually pretty easy. I'm their pitcher, and we're playing in the championship game."

Erin's jaw practically hit the ground, and her ice cream was forgotten.

"You have to be kidding me," she said.

"It's the truth. I told them my name was Johnny. I even hung out at William's house and ate pizza with the team after one of the games."

"This is crazy," Erin said, and I couldn't tell how she felt about it, so I continued to try to explain myself.

"It was the only solution I could think of. I love to play baseball. When I found out Chester didn't have a girls' team, I figured out the next-best option."

"And that happened to be dressing up like a boy? What about playing for Riverside? I thought that was the solution the town came up with."

"I promised my dad I'd play for Chester, just like he did when he was my age," I told her. "And it worked. But now things are a big mess. That's why I need your help."

"How in the world can I help?"

"I change before and after each game in the bathroom at the park, and about a week ago I walked in and Jessa was there. I still had the team uniform on, and it only took her a few seconds to figure out what I've been doing. Now she's threatening to tell everyone unless I do what she wants."

"Why am I not surprised? That's the type of person she is."

"It doesn't look like she's going to change her mind. I'm out of the game unless I listen to her."

"What is it she wants you to do?"

"It's not only me. It's both of us. She wants the two of us to drop out of the pageant."

"Why would she want us to do that?"

"She sees us as a threat. Especially you."

Erin laughed so hard, she snorted, which would have had me cracking up if things hadn't been so serious. "Yeah, right. I'm the last person she should be worried about."

"You're good, Erin. Mom says it all the time. You have a chance to win, and Jessa sees that."

"I don't believe that for a second, but that only makes

me want to try harder to win. It would be so good to see the look on Jessa's face if she didn't win."

"Here's the thing . . . ," I began, and even though I knew that once the words left my mouth, I'd never ever be able to take them back, I couldn't stop. "I have to play in the championship game. I promised my dad I would."

"But Jessa's going to tell everyone about you," Erin said.

"There's a way to stop her."

Erin didn't understand what I was getting at for a moment, but as soon as she figured it out, her face changed. Her eyes narrowed and she frowned.

"You're asking me to quit, aren't you?"

"I don't know what else to do."

"Seriously? After all the work we've done?"

"I can't let her expose me. It'll ruin everything. I won't get to play ball."

"Right. Kind of like how I won't be able to compete in the pageant."

"It's awful to even ask," I said, because it was, but I was desperate.

"It is." Erin's voice had a mean, hard edge to it. "I thought we were friends."

"That's why I thought I could ask—"

"No. Stop right there," Erin said, and cut me off. "A friend wouldn't do that. It's not fair to put this all on me. The pageant is important to me. Just like baseball is to you."

"I'm sorry. I didn't mean to make you feel like you had to quit."

"But you did. That's the problem. You wouldn't have said anything if you didn't want me to make that choice." Erin stood up and dumped the rest of her cone into the trashcan behind us.

"What did you do that for?" I asked.

"I lost my appetite. I have to go home," she said, her voice now cool and even. She began to walk away, and then stopped. "And that thing about playing on the boys' team. What you did wasn't right. They're counting on you, and when it comes out that you've been lying and can't play in the championship game, you're going to let every single one of your teammates down."

"I didn't mean to lie to any of you. I only wanted to play ball."

"But you did lie, and I trusted you, Gabby. But I guess that was my first mistake, because it turns out you've been lying about a lot of things."

"Not on purpose," I said, trying to reason with her.

"You don't lie by accident," she said. "But now I'm walking away. On purpose."

She stormed through the crowd of people lined up for ice cream. Everyone was happy and joking with each other, but I stood there feeling awful. I threw the rest of my cone into the same wastebasket. I'd messed up big-time. And that was the truth.

COACH MARSHALL WANTED ONE MORE PRACTICE
before the championship game, to make sure we were in
top-notch shape. The problem was, I was nowhere near
being ready. He split us into two teams to scrimmage, and
I was a disaster. I couldn't focus on anything but Erin and
Jessa and the mess I'd made. I walked two players in a
row and let a runner come home when I missed a simple
pop-up. And that was all in the first inning.

After another horrendous inning, with the boys
around me grumbling under their breath about my pitching, Coach Marshall pulled me aside.

"What's going on in that head of yours?" He tapped
me on the top of my hat, and for a second I was afraid

he might pull it off and reveal everything. "The person I'm seeing on the pitcher's mound isn't the Johnny I've known all season."

"I'm sorry. I guess I'm too focused on the championship. I'm letting the pressure get to me," I said, because I couldn't very well tell him what was really happening. He was right. My head was a disaster. I couldn't stop thinking about the giant mess I'd made with all my lies. The last thing I had wanted to do was make Erin mad, but after I called four times last night and she refused to talk to me, I knew it wasn't going to be easy to make things right with her.

"We can't have you stress about the game. We're counting on you to pitch, so you need to make sure you can do that. Can I depend on you?"

I was afraid to meet his eyes, because I didn't want to show him how serious things were. I scanned the field, where half of my team waited to start the next inning. I glanced at the bench, where the other half sat, including Owen, one of the best catchers I've ever played with. This was my team now; I owed it to them to get myself together and help them win.

I met Coach Marshall's gaze and tried to muster up

as much confidence as I could. "You can count on me. I'm ready to win it all."

He pointed at me. "Good. Now remember that when you're on the pitcher's mound. Show me you're ready to help lead the team to victory."

I gave him a thumbs-up and jogged onto the field. I tossed the ball into my glove, the familiar sound of leather reminding me how much I loved the game.

Strong, steady, strike, I told myself.

I could do this.

I would do this.

No, I had to do this.

And not for the team or Dad but for myself.

I COULDN'T SLEEP. I TOSSED AND TURNED, AND EVERY
time I began to drift off, my mind kept returning to the
giant mess I'd created that I had no idea how to fix.

After an hour I got up and headed downstairs. Mom
swore by her warm milk at night, so I thought I'd give
it a try. But when I reached the kitchen, I discovered I
wasn't the only one who was still awake. Grandma sat at
the table with her hands wrapped around a steaming cup
of tea.

"Can't sleep?" she asked.

"How'd you guess?"

"Well, I'm pretty sure you didn't come down here to
do the dishes."

I laughed, despite my mood. "You're right about that. I was going to make some warm milk."

"I'll do it," Grandma said, and stood up. She pulled a painted mug down out of the cupboard and filled it before putting it into the microwave.

When she brought it to me, I picked the mug up and inspected it. It was hand-painted bright yellow and had white and red polka dots all over it. In sloppy black paint the word "Mom" was written.

"This is an interesting use of polka dots," I said.

"You made it when you were in third grade. It's one of my favorites."

I vaguely remembered selecting the colors and probably getting paint all over the place in the process. "Third grade? This looks more like something Ava would make."

Grandma laughed. "Well, if I recall, you made it at the arts and crafts booth during the Corn Festival. And about halfway through, a group of kids started a game of baseball, so you raced to finish the mug so you could play with them."

"That sounds like something I'd do." I ran my fingers over the mug. "I remember the kids were older, but I was determined to keep up with them. And instead of telling me I couldn't play, Dad encouraged me."

"He always cheered you on," Grandma said.

"I wish he was here cheering me on right now."

"We all do."

"I miss him so bad." I didn't even try to hide the sadness in my voice.

"Is that what's keeping you up?" she asked gently.

I took a sip of the milk, and it warmed my insides when I swallowed. "That and a whole long list of other things."

"Do you want to talk about it?"

I did, but how could I? I wished I could spill my guts and come clean, but that was pretty much impossible unless I wanted to deal with the consequences. I decided to talk to her by being vague.

"I'm nervous about the pageant. I love the dress you made, and Mom's been working so hard with me, but it still doesn't feel right. When we ran through everything at the rehearsal, it was like I was acting and pretending to be someone totally different from who I am. What good is it if the person up onstage isn't really me?"

"It's not any good at all," Grandma said. "And your mom would agree with me."

"I doubt it. She's worked so hard to turn me into her version of a pageant girl."

"And she'll realize how wrong she was the moment you step onto the stage. Think about the day you went dress shopping."

I groaned. "I'd rather not."

"Of course you wouldn't, because your mom tried to put you into dresses that weren't right for you. And then what happened?"

"You made me the perfect dress." I pictured it hanging in my closet. I had tried it on a few more times just because I loved it, and I couldn't wait to wear that dress.

"And your mom saw how right it was for you."

"She did, didn't she?"

"And she'll see how right everything else is too if you show your true self in the pageant. Forget the way you think you're supposed to walk or talk or smile. What you're supposed to do isn't going to make you unique. You'll be standing up there with all the girls who are doing the exact same thing. In order to stand out, you simply need to be yourself."

"I don't know . . . ," I said hesitantly.

"I *do* know," Grandma said. "The person you are is pretty incredible, and she deserves to be the one standing in front of everyone in the pageant. Your mom can't argue with that."

"Thanks," I told her, and gave her a giant hug. Maybe I'd been pretending around everyone else, but Grandma saw me for who I was, and that made all the difference.

"You're a brilliant girl," Grandma whispered. "All you have to do is be that girl."

I headed upstairs feeling warm and fuzzy inside from both the milk and Grandma's advice.

What she said made sense. All summer long I'd been hiding my true self from everyone . . . Mom, Erin, the baseball team, even Dad. How was that fair? I'd already hurt one person. How many more would I hurt if I kept this up?

I walked to the mirror, the same one I'd stood in front of when I'd made the decision to join the boys' baseball team. This time, though, I didn't have my hair pulled back or a hat on or one of Mom's awful pageant dresses on. I saw a girl in an old softball T-shirt and messy hair. I had a scrape on my knee from sliding into third base a few days ago, and the lime-green nail polish on my toes was chipped. And for the first time in a long time, I recognized myself.

Maybe the solution was always the truth.

A plan began to form in my mind. It was risky. Very

risky. It could cost me both the pageant and the championship game. And I'd need Owen's help if I wanted to pull it off. But after everything that had happened, it was a risk I needed to take, because being honest with myself and those around me was the most important thing.

IT WAS THE MORNING OF THE PAGEANT AND THE championship game, but you would've thought it was Christmas by the way Mom acted.

"Wake up, sleepyhead, wake up," she yelled as she bounced on my bed with Ava in her arms. Mom's hair was in curlers and her face was all made up even thought it was still pretty much the crack of dawn. One of her signature smoothies sat on the nightstand.

I was exhausted, and no amount of milk could have helped the night before. I was up late into the night worrying about my plan. Owen had agreed to help, but that didn't mean it would work. I didn't trust Jessa at all and had been on guard waiting for her to strike. And I'd bet my baseball signed by the Indians that she wouldn't leave me alone when I showed up at the pageant.

"I hope you're ready for today," Mom said. "It's going to be an amazing one."

"As ready as I can be," I told her.

Ava snuggled under my covers with me, and Mom walked to the closet, where my outfits for the pageant hung. She unzipped the bag that held them and caressed my dress lovingly.

"You'll be amazing," she told me. "You've worked hard for this."

My plan flashed through my mind, and I felt a twinge of guilt. Mom might have been happy with me now, but I wasn't so sure how she'd feel after the pageant was over.

Grandma made a giant breakfast of pancakes, eggs, and bacon, but I was too nervous to do much more than nibble on a piece of bacon and pick at my eggs. Mom chatted excitedly about the upcoming day, and I tried to act like everything was okay. I thought I did a good job at it, up until we arrived backstage and I spotted Jessa.

She stood in front of a mirror with a curling iron, fixing her hair even though it already looked flawless.

When she saw me, she frowned. She put her curling

iron down and came over. I pictured a snake slithering toward its prey, and I took a step closer to Mom as if she could protect me.

"Hi, Gabby and Mrs. Ryan," she said, her voice all friendly and sweet, but she didn't fool me. "I didn't expect to see you backstage."

"I was helping Gabby drop her stuff off, and then I'll be sitting front and center in the audience," Mom said, completely unaware that it wasn't her that Jessa was saying she was surprised to see.

"How nice," she said, and turned to me. "What about you, Gabby? Will your friend Johnny be joining your mother in the audience?"

My stomach lurched in fear, and I tried not to throw up. This was not happening. Not here. Not now.

"Whose Johnny?" Mom asked, puzzled.

"Oh, you haven't met him yet?" Jessa asked. "He and Gabby are close. Very close. I'm surprised she hasn't told you about him. But I have a feeling he'll be at the pageant today. In fact, I'm positive he'll show up."

"You'll have to introduce him to me," Mom said, and I mumbled some kind of lame reply that might have made it sound like I would.

"I'll let you two get set up. It was nice to see you, Mrs. Ryan. And good luck, Gabby. May the best man—whoops, I mean, woman, win today!" She gave a little wave and headed back to her station.

"Johnny?" Mom asked, her eyebrow raised.

"It's nothing," I told her. "Jessa has no idea what she's talking about."

Mom opened her mouth, most likely to argue about this boy I had been hanging out with, but thankfully Mrs. Sylvan clapping her hands together saved me.

"Okay, girls. We have thirty minutes until the pageant starts. Now is the time to make sure you have everything and complete any last-minute touch-ups before you march your beautiful selves across the stage. We'll be lining up in fifteen minutes for the opening."

"That's my cue to leave," Mom said. She stepped back and took a long look at me. Before we had left the house, she had straightened my hair and put a special spray on it to make it all silky and shiny. I'd let her put a small amount of makeup on me, enough to make my "eyes pop," according to her, and some tinted lip gloss and blush. Her eyes welled up. "I'm so proud of you, honey. You're beautiful, both inside and out."

"Thanks, Mom."

She adjusted the collar on the yellow shirt all the girls would wear for the opening introductions. LaMarca's Farm, the largest producer of corn in the area, sponsored the pageant and provided the shirts. The front of the shirts had a giant number fifty, for the Corn Festival's anniversary, and the farm's slogan, "I pop for corn from LaMarca's," was on the back. If that wasn't embarrassing enough, we wore the shirts with bright green shorts, so basically we all looked like giant stalks of corn. I couldn't believe girls in this town went crazy over all of this; my friends would have fallen over laughing if they could have seen me.

"You're going to wow them today," Mom said as she gave me a close once-over to make sure I looked okay.

"I hope so," I told her, and wow them I would if all went according to plan, just not in the way Mom envisioned.

She left to go sit with Grandma and Ava, and I set up my stuff and ran to join everyone who was already waiting backstage. Erin stood with Nina and Alexa, two girls she went to school with. I caught her eye and gave her a small wave, but she quickly turned away. I felt a sharp pain in my chest because I was the one who had hurt her and I deserved her anger. But if my plan worked today, maybe I could make it up to her.

"You better know what you're doing," Jessa hissed into my ear, coming up behind me.

But before I could say anything back, Mrs. Sylvan ushered Jessa and me into our spots in line.

The rest of the girls were already lined up when I got to them. Hannah and Ellia, the two girls I stood between, moved to make room for me. Ellia's face was as white as a ghost, and she looked so nervous that I was afraid she might puke right then. It made me feel a tiny bit better that at least I wasn't the only one who was terrified to go out onstage.

"All right, girls, this is it. Get your pageant faces on!" Mrs. Sylvan chirped in a way-too-cheerful voice. She gave us an exaggerated smile to show how we should look, and then stepped aside as one by one each of the age groups took their place under the bright lights and introduced themselves. The line moved so fast, I didn't have time to panic about Jessa, and soon it was my turn. I took a deep breath and summoned all the courage I could before stepping onto the stage. Ready or not, I was about to put my plan into action.

THE FIRST PART OF THE PAGEANT WENT OFF WITHOUT a hitch. I didn't trip when I walked out onstage to introduce myself. My interview question, "What is your favorite subject in school and why?" was a lot easier than any of the ones Mom had Erin and me practice, which meant I was able to talk about how much I love gym, without stuttering or sounding like an idiot. But no matter how smoothly things were going, my mind wandered to those hot humid summer nights when we'd watch the lightning in the distance. Grandma called it "the calm before the storm," because usually within the hour the skies would open up in a downpour and rage and drench the ground. The introduction and interview portion of the pageant were my calm before the storm, because Hurricane Jessa struck right before the formal wear competition.

After rocking my interview question, I ran backstage to change into my dress. I couldn't wait to wear it. Except, when I pulled it out of my locker, the bottom was covered in thick greasy streaks, and on the ground was my tube of eye black. Someone must have gone through my bag, which held not only my pageant stuff but my baseball gear, too.

"This can't be happening," I moaned. My beautiful perfect dress Grandma had spent a ton of time on was destroyed. I couldn't go out onstage in it; the judges would think I was making a joke of the pageant. I slid down the side of the locker and sat on the floor, the ruined dress in my lap. Girls ran around behind me, making last-minute touches to their own outfits, but I didn't move. How could I? I no longer had anything to wear.

"Oh wow," Jessa said, appearing beside me. "That's a really unique choice for the formal wear competition. Very daring with the design on the bottom."

She had changed into the green dress we had both tried on that day in the dressing room. And surprise,

surprise, it looked amazing. Her hair was pulled into a side bun, with curls falling around her face. I had no idea how she could look so pretty on the outside but be so mean on the inside.

"You did this," I said, and fought the urge to cry. I wouldn't give Jessa the satisfaction.

"Did what?"

"Why do you hate me?" I asked her. "My mom could work with me twenty-four hours a day, and I'd still never stand a chance at winning. I was only doing this for her. I thought it would give her something to focus on so she wouldn't miss my dad so much."

"You don't get it. Your mom's a legacy. That fact alone will get the judges' attention. And it's not fair that Erin has gotten the same tips you have from your mom. I've trained for years to prepare for this pageant, and you simply visit here and make friends with Erin, and now the judges love both of you. Things don't work that way. So while you think it's only fun, this is serious business for some of us."

Maybe Jessa believed that, but she was wrong. To most of us, this was fun, the way it was supposed to be. I thought back to all the moments when Erin and I would laugh and joke while practicing. And then I remembered the other day when Jessa's mom had yelled at her in the parking lot. Mom had pressured me to compete in the pageant because she loved it so much, but maybe Jessa's mom put a different kind of pressure on her.

"It's time to line up and show the crowd how beautiful you look," Mrs. Sylvan trilled, interrupting the two of us.

"See you onstage," Jessa said, and glanced down at my dress. "Mrs. Sylvan is right. You do look very, um, beautiful."

The space cleared out, and I was left alone. This was it, I thought. I couldn't go onstage in this dress. My plan was over, and Jessa had won in some kind of invisible battle I hadn't even entered.

Mom would worry when I didn't walk out with everyone else, so I should probably leave and explain. I packed my stuff into my bag and was almost done when I heard footsteps behind me. I tensed up and assumed it was Jessa, back to do some other awful thing.

But when I turned around, it wasn't Jessa; it was Erin.

She wore a pale yellow dress with diamond rhinestones across the chest and on the straps. The color was perfect for her red hair, which was loose around her shoulders, and she had tiny gold star-shaped earrings that sparkled in the overhead lights.

"What are you doing here?" I asked. "You're going to miss the competition."

"No, *we're* going to miss the competition. We need to get out there before our age group is called."

"I can't compete," I told her. I held up my dress. "It's ruined. Jessa did it."

"I know," she said. "I heard her bragging about it to her friend Jocelyn when we were in line. We can't let her get away with this." She reached out her hand. "Here, let me have it. I have an idea."

I handed the dress to her, and she ran to her locker, where she pulled out a pair of scissors and began to cut the bottom of it.

"What are you doing?" I yelled.

"Fixing your dress. Trust me. I have some safety pins we'll use for the hem. No one will ever have any idea that Jessa tried to ruin it."

I waited anxiously while she worked. Through the speakers I heard the group of five-year-olds through eight-year-olds being called. It wouldn't be long before it was time for the group of nine-year-olds through twelve-year-olds.

"Forget about me," I told Erin. "If you don't get out there, you're going to miss your chance."

"We'll make it. I have one more pin and it'll be ready to go." She fiddled with the hem and then handed the dress to me. "Here, put it on."

Without pausing to see what it looked like, I simply pulled the dress over my head and let her zip it up.

"Hurry!" I rushed toward the door leading to the stage. I didn't care if I made it in time, but I didn't want Erin to miss out. Not after how hard she had worked.

"Wait." Erin grabbed me by the shoulders. She turned me around in front of the full-length mirror that hung by the door, for those girls who wanted to do last-minute prep. "Take a look at yourself."

I paused in front of the mirror. The dress was a lot shorter than before, and instead of a straight hem, Erin had pinned it up in little bunches, so it curled under, which meant that any sign of Jessa's sabotage was gone. The way the fabric was arranged made the dress poof out around the bottom in a unique and really cool way.

"This is amazing," I told her.

"Not too shabby, huh?" She grinned. "And it looks great with your shoes."

I wiggled my toes in my Converse. "They do make the outfit, don't they?"

"It's the perfect look for you."

"Thanks," I told her, and then I got serious. "Listen, I'm sorry about—"

She held her hand up, signaling for me to stop. "Not now. I'm still mad at you, but this isn't the time to talk about it. We have to get out there, or we are going to let Jessa win, which is something I'm not about to let happen."

We ran out of the changing room, my skirt brushing against my knees. I couldn't wait to see the look on Jessa's face when I stepped onto the stage and rocked my dress.

39

I HELD UP THE SHORTS AND SPARKLY TANK TOP MOM had bought for me to wear for the talent portion. I stuck my tongue out at the awful outfit and wished Jessa could have ruined this instead of my dress. Not that it would have mattered, though, because I didn't plan on wearing it. I pulled out my baseball uniform and put it on. I tucked my hair under my hat like I had all summer long and took what was left of the eye black and made thick lines under my eyes. I grabbed my small duffel bag and was ready to go.

I snuck over to the high school boy who was in charge of the audio for the talent portion. He was on his phone texting and barely looked up when I stood in front of him.

"Hey, I'm Gabby Ryan. When it's my turn, don't turn my music on, okay? I'm going to do something different."

"Yeah, sure, whatever," he said, barely taking his eyes off his phone.

I headed to the group of girls who waited on the side of the stage and held tightly to my bag. A few of them gave me odd looks, but thankfully no one commented. I was too nervous to talk to anyone and was afraid I'd chicken out if I did. One by one each of the girls ahead of me did their talent, until there was only one more girl before me. Her name was Amelia and she did a dance so perfect and flawless that I was relieved I wouldn't be following her with the routine Mom had had me learn. The audience would think I was doing a comedy act compared to how incredible Amelia was.

"Next up, we have Gabby Ryan," the local radio host, who was the announcer for the pageant, told the crowd. "She will be dancing to a classic song from the 1950s."

The audience cheered as I walked across the stage. To say I was terrified would be putting it mildly; my legs shook and felt all wobbly. But I needed to do this if I had any shot of fixing things.

I waited off to the side as Owen climbed the steps in

his baseball uniform too. He walked to the other end of the stage and squatted down, his glove poised and ready for my first pitch.

The audience was silent. There was no cheering or talking as they tried to figure out what I was about to do. I pulled three balls out of my duffel bag and set two on the ground. Maybe I wouldn't be able to pitch in the championship game for Dad, but here, on this stage in the pageant Mom loved so much, I could show everyone what he had taught me. And so I let the first pitch go and smiled as it landed with a satisfying *thunk* in Owen's glove.

That would have totally been a strike, I thought.

I picked up the second ball, signaled to Owen that I'd be throwing a fastball, and let it fly. Again, it hit dead center in his glove.

At this point, there was a low buzz among everyone. They were talking about me. And who wouldn't? I was probably confusing the heck out of them, but I didn't care.

I envisioned myself not on the stage but on the pitcher's mound in the bottom of the ninth, when all we needed was one more out to win the game. And when the pitch crosses the plate, the batter swings and misses, and the crowd goes wild!

I picked up the last ball and got into position to throw Dad's infamous curveball, the first pitch he ever taught me. I pulled my arm back, wound up, and let go.

I did it! I fulfilled my promise to Dad. Because it isn't where you are that matters, but who you are. And right now, onstage, I was Gabby, the girl who loved baseball, and I wasn't going to let anyone stop me from being myself.

I gave Owen a thumbs-up, and he mouthed "Great job" as he left the stage. He didn't know the second part of my plan, but I'd told him it might mean I wouldn't be able to play in the championship game.

I walked to the podium, where the announcer stood and stared at me as if I'd just walked out onstage and spoken in an alien language. I guess throwing a baseball during a beauty pageant isn't too far off from that.

"Do you mind if I say something?" I whispered to her.

"Um, sure, I guess," she said, and stepped aside.

I stood in front of the microphone for a moment and gazed at the crowd who had directed their complete attention at me. I repeated Dad's mantra to myself.

Strong, steady, strike.

"Hi," I said, and my voice echoed back through the

sound system. I spotted my family a few rows back from the front, and Mom watched me, puzzled but not upset, which was a good sign. I gave her a weak smile. "My talent today was supposed to be a dance number I'd been working on all summer. But trust me, even with all the practice I've had, you don't want that. I look more like a hippo on roller skates than a dancer."

There were a few laughs from the crowd, which gave me the courage to keep talking.

"My true talent this past summer has been lying," I confessed. "I've been pretending to be someone I'm not. My dad is serving overseas, which has been hard for my whole family. I agreed to compete in the pageant because I wanted to make my mom happy. And it has, and that's more important than anything else. But what I love to do is play softball. My dad taught me everything about it. It's our thing. But then I found out there wasn't a girls' team in Chester because everyone was more interested in the pageant. I get it, we all have things we like to do, and I could've joined Riverside's team, but I couldn't imagine not playing for the team my dad once played on."

This was it. The point of no return. I tried to calm my nerves, took a deep breath, and let the truth fly.

"So I signed up for Chester's team. I pulled my hair back under my hat and called myself Johnny. And I was good. *Really* good. I pitched and struck out player after player, which proves girls are as good as boys."

I let my voice get just a little bit quieter, as if to let the audience in on a secret. "And I'm pretty sure I proved that sometimes girls can be even better."

I spotted a bunch of women in the audience smiling or nodding in agreement, which was the encouragement I needed to finish my speech.

"But that was the problem. I wasn't playing as a girl. And I'm tired of hiding who I am. I don't want to be Johnny anymore. I want to be Gabby. And if that means I won't be able to pitch in the championship game, then I guess it's the price I'll have to pay. Because I've learned it's a lot better to be yourself than someone you aren't. So I'm sorry to anyone I've lied to or hurt. And I promise that it's over now."

The words spilled out, and I was surprised at not only how easy it was to tell the truth, but also how good it felt.

"Thank you," I said, not sure how to end my big confession. I made my way toward the side of the stage, ready to get yelled at by Mrs. Sylvan or to have Jessa gloat in my face about how I'd ruined my chances at winning. But then I heard someone start to clap. A single set of hands clapping for me. I searched out the crowd, and there, standing on her feet, was Mom. She wiped tears away from her eyes and blew me a kiss. Grandma stood and began to clap too, and slowly, one by one, other people in the audience brought their hands together. They were all applauding me, and it wasn't because I was the prettiest or most talented or answered my interview question well, but it was because I was myself. I was Gabby Ryan.

IT PROBABLY COMES AS NO BIG SURPRISE THAT I
wasn't crowned Miss Popcorn. Instead Erin was the winner in our age group, and the expression of pure happiness on her face when she found out gave me the best
feeling in the world. She was in shock when her name
was announced and kept pointing at herself and mouth-
ing "Me." The audience couldn't help but laugh at how
cute she was. Because even if she didn't recognize it, we
all knew she was the perfect choice.

Jessa, on the other hand, pitched a fit backstage,
throwing things and talking to her friend Livia about how
unfair it was because Erin didn't even know the proper
way to breathe when you competed. I made a mental

note to ask Mom about that one, because I had no idea there were multiple ways to breathe.

I tried to talk to Erin backstage after the pageant, but she had a big group of girls around her, all of them congratulating her and touching the traditional Miss Popcorn crown made out of woven corn husks, exactly like the three Mom had sitting on her bookshelf.

Jessa found me as I zipped my bag full of my pageant gear. This time, though, I wasn't nervous to talk to her and stood my ground.

"Wow, talk about pathetic. I mean, how desperate do you have to be to pull that little stunt onstage for the talent competition? Too bad it didn't work," she said smugly.

I refused to back down and faced her head-on. "Actually, it was the right thing to do, which you wouldn't understand, after trying to ruin my dress. Now, that's desperate."

"Whatever. You still didn't win," she shot back.

"No, the person who deserved to win did. Erin was amazing, and you never stood a chance next to her."

"Please, I was a million times better than both of you," Jessa said, and stormed off mumbling about the crazy judges and how they would have no idea how to pick a winner even if she was standing right in front of them.

As I headed out of the backstage area, I spotted Erin outside and waved my hand to get her attention. I wanted—no, needed—to make things up to her. I'd apologize over and over again forever if it meant she'd forgive me. But before I could try to tell her how sorry I was, a man with a camera and a hat that said JASPER COUNTY WEEKLY NEWS grabbed her. I wasn't about to interrupt her interview, so I searched the crowd until I found my family at a picnic table.

Mom jumped up and wrapped me in her arms.

"You're not mad?" I asked, my face smooshed against her chest.

"How could I be? That was so brave of you." Mom put her hand on my shoulder. "Talking in front of everybody like that."

"How was that brave? It would have been brave of me to have never lied."

"Not necessarily. It's always harder to admit you're wrong, which is exactly what you did."

"I guess that's true," I agreed. "And it sure wasn't easy, but I needed to do it."

"And I do too," Mom said. "I was wrong and I'm sorry."

"About what?" I asked, confused.

"Pushing you to do the pageant. Trying to make you into something you weren't. I got carried away with the excitement and didn't even stop to consider that the person I was teaching you to be was nothing like the daughter I love."

"It's okay," I told her, and it was. "Besides, I liked spending all that time with you."

"So you really wanted to play baseball, huh?"

"Yeah, about that . . ."

"I should be mad at you and be a good parent and punish you for deceiving everyone, but I have to admit that I'm impressed. You fooled a whole team of boys."

"Not only did I fool them," I said, "I struck most of them out, too!"

"You go, girl," Mom said, and high-fived me.

"I wanted to tell you," I said. "But I had no idea how you'd react, so I didn't want to take the chance and not be able to play, especially after I promised Dad I would."

"He would've understood if you couldn't have played."

"But I *wanted* to play. For the city of Chester." I looked down at the ground and scuffed at the dirt with my shoe. "It's going to sound stupid, but I felt like keeping my promise to Dad would help bring him home. As if he was counting on me to do this one good thing, and if I could, everything would be okay."

"I can understand that. It makes sense," Mom said.

"I don't sound silly?"

"Believe me, every night I make promises to the universe to keep him safe. We love your father and don't want to feel helpless, so we do things that make us feel like we're helping. Does that make sense?"

"It does," I told her. And then shyly I said, "Do you know what else helps?"

"What's that, sweetie?"

"Talking about it. Just hearing you say this now makes me feel better. We never talk about Dad not being here. I've felt like I've been keeping everything bottled up since he left, and I don't want to do that."

"Oh, Gabby, I don't want to do that either. I'm sorry if I've made you feel that way."

"I miss him so much," I told Mom. "Sometimes my heart hurts thinking about him being away."

"So do I." Mom paused for a moment and played with her earring.

I watched the clouds race past and thought about how even though Mom could get pageant-obsessed and be supergirly, the two of us weren't much different.

"I have an idea," Mom said. "What if instead of our daily runs, we take daily walks? And we can use the time to talk about Dad whenever you want to."

"Can we take these walks after dinner to Coneheads?" I joked.

"That sounds wonderful," Mom said, and it did. It truly did.

She gestured toward the baseball field, where crowds of people were headed. "Now, I believe you have a championship game to pitch in."

"They're not going to let me play," I said, a tight pull in my chest at losing out on what I'd been working so hard for all summer. "But I'd better go tell them the truth too."

I needed to complete the final part of my plan, although it might mean losing out on the one thing that had meant the most to me this summer. It was time for Johnny to say good-bye, even if that meant Gabby wasn't allowed on the team.

THE BLEACHERS FOR THE MIDDLE SCHOOL DIVISION OF
the championship game were as full as the audience
had been for the pageant. Everyone wanted to see if
the Chester rec center boys could stay undefeated, or if
Bolton Village would finally stop them.

My teammates were in left field, sitting in a circle as
Coach Marshall talked to them. I still had my uniform on
and hair up. I looked like I belonged, but it was time to
let them know that I didn't.

Owen noticed me first and gave me a quick wave.
The rest of the boys turned, and soon everyone's attention was focused on me, including Coach Marshall's. I
wanted to slow down and delay the inevitable, but I owed

it to the team to tell them everything now so that Coach Marshall had time to decide who would pitch.

"Hi, guys," I said when I reached the group. The shaky feeling came back as I tried to figure out what was going through everyone's minds, but their faces didn't give anything away. How many of them had been at the pageant and already knew Johnny didn't exist?

I took a deep breath and began to talk. "I have something I need to tell you. And you'll probably hate me for it, because I'm going to let you all down, which is the last thing I want to do. You've been such awesome teammates. But the thing is, Johnny doesn't exist. That's not my name. My real name is Gabby, which means I shouldn't even be playing on your team, because I'm a girl."

Some of the boys in the group shifted around and looked at each other, and I told myself to be brave and keep on going with the full truth.

"When I came here this summer, I couldn't wait to play softball. I love summer and being out on the field, so when I found out the city of Chester didn't have a girls' team this year, I was devastated. I didn't know what to do. I couldn't imagine not playing, so I created Johnny. And Johnny was good. His whole team was good, and he loved them and couldn't wait to make it to the championship. And that's why I feel awful about pretending to be someone I'm not. Because now I can't play in the game, and I've let you all down when you counted on me."

I waited for them to react, for someone to yell at me or say something about what a liar I'd been, but no one said a word.

Finally Coach Marshall spoke up. "You're one of the best pitchers I've ever seen. For a boy or a girl. And while I wish you had been honest with us, I understand why you weren't. In fact, all the boys on the team do. We talked about it before you came."

"You were talking about me?" I asked.

"It's all anyone is talking about, the girl with the awesome pitching arm in the pageant. And what I didn't understand, Owen filled me in on. He explained everything to the whole team, and what you did makes sense. Every one of us is here because we love baseball and would be crushed if someone told us we couldn't play. Most of us would've done exactly what you did if we had to."

"I didn't mean to ruin things," I said. "I just wanted to play ball."

"It's okay. We'll forgive you. Right, team?" he asked the group, and the boys all nodded. "But you'll need to make it up to us, and I know exactly how you can do that."

"Yes, of course," I said, glad the team wasn't chasing me with pitchforks, ready for a fight.

"You need to promise to help us win the championship game."

"Oh, you can bet I'll be cheering louder than anyone else from the stands," I told him.

"No," Coach Marshall said. "I mean when you pitch. I'm expecting you to keep striking out batters like you did all summer."

"You want me to pretend to be Johnny? I'd do anything for the team, but I can't keep lying."

"We kicked Johnny off the team," Coach said. "We hope our new pitcher is a girl named Gabby."

"But how?" I asked. "This is a boys' team."

"Right after Owen helped you with the pageant, he came and told me everything that had been happening. I checked the rules, and there's nowhere that says a girl can't play on a boys' team, so I talked to the Corn Festival committee, and they agreed that since there isn't a girls' team for you to join, it's only fair to allow you to keep playing with us. So what do you say? Want to help the city of Chester win this championship?"

"Is everyone okay with it?" I asked, not wanting to get too excited.

"We wouldn't be able to win this without you," Georgie said.

"Yeah, you helped us get this far. Now you need to help us finish and take home the championship," Zach agreed.

Calvin stood up. "While I hate to admit I got struck out by a girl, you pitch as good as any boy I've ever seen."

"She's pitched better than any *boy* you've ever seen," Owen told him. "And don't make it sound like she only struck you out once; I seem to remember catching multiple strikes she threw your way."

"Okay, okay, you're right," Calvin said with a sheepish grin. "You're good, Gabby. We'd be nuts not to let you keep playing with us."

The rest of the boys nodded in agreement.

"Then I guess I have to win this game to make it up to you," I said, and I had never been so happy to apologize to anyone in my life.

"I like that plan," Coach Marshall said. "Now, boys . . . and girl, this is the game we've all been working toward. I have no doubt you can crush Bolton Village, so get out there and make it happen!"

We crowded around him to say our chant like we did before every game. I put my hand in the middle of the group, and the boys piled theirs on top of mine. My hand didn't look any different from anyone else's. In fact, it looked as if it belonged there.

I FOLLOWED THE TEAM TO THE BENCH AND SAT IN THE
middle of everyone, and no one said a word about the
girl on the bench. We cheered as AJ walked up to bat
first and made it to second with a double. The next two
players struck out, but Georgie got on base. Calvin was
up next, and I was all set to cheer as loudly as I could,
when someone tapped me on the shoulder.

Was this it? Was it all too good to be true? I had a
feeling this was when I was going to be told I couldn't
play in the game.

But the person standing there wasn't some mean
angry-looking umpire or parent ready to kick me off the
team. It was Mom. And she was on her phone.

"What are you doing?" I whispered, so I wouldn't draw attention to us. Why was Mom coming to talk to me in front of the team in the middle of an inning? That wasn't exactly the way to fit in with a bench full of boys.

"I have a very important person on the line."

"Um, okay." I tried to catch Grandma's eye to send her a secret message to come and pull my crazy mom back into the stands, but she was busy with Ava and wasn't looking my way.

"And he asked to speak to you. I mean, if you're busy, I could tell your dad to call back—"

"Wait, what? Dad's on the phone? Of course I want to talk to him!"

Mom laughed and held the phone out to me.

"Daddy? Is it really you?" I asked, because this was incredible.

"It's me, Curveball!" he said, and the whole world disappeared and it was as if it were only the two of us in our backyard at home talking as we played catch.

"I can't believe you called," I said.

"You didn't think I'd miss out on your big night. I heard a rumor that a certain girl I know was going to pitch in the championship game."

"Just like you did," I told him.

"Strong, steady, strike," Dad said, and it didn't feel as if he were a million miles away. It felt as if he was right here with me, cheering me on.

"I wouldn't have made it to this point if it wasn't for you," I said, and I felt a familiar tug in my heart. I missed Dad so much.

"I may have helped you learn how to pitch, but you're the one who became the amazing young woman I'm so proud of," he said, and I could feel it. The strength of his love wrapped around me as if he were giving me a hug from all the way on the other side of the world. He was with me even when he wasn't.

"Gabby, it's time!" Coach Marshall yelled from the other end of the bench.

"You've got this," Dad said. "Don't ever doubt yourself for a moment."

"I love you," I said, and I didn't care who heard it.

"Right back at you, Curveball," Dad said. "Now go throw some strikes and win yourself a trophy!"

I passed the phone back to Mom and jogged to the pitcher's mound as the rest of the team took the field. I turned around in a slow circle and tried to take it all in.

I was here, pitching in the championship game like I'd promised Dad, and I was doing it as myself, not someone I pretended to be.

I scanned the bleachers and found Erin sitting with her mom. She had her crown on and held a giant sign. *Gabby, Gabby, she's our WOman. If she can't win it, no one can!* was printed across it in red letters. When she saw me, she smiled and gave me a thumbs-up.

I gave her one right back. I still had a ways to go to make things up to her, but this was a start.

Time seemed to stand still as I stood on the pitcher's mound, like I'd done hundreds of times before. I spun the ball around and around in my hand and thought about everything that had brought me to this moment—Mom's endless support, Grandma's pep talks, Maddie and my team at home, Owen and my team here, Erin, and Dad. Always Dad. And as much as this game was for him, it was also for everyone else who believed in me, and I was so lucky to have every one of them in my life.

Bolton Village's batter stepped up to the plate, and the crowd went wild. Owen signaled a pitch to me and I nodded. It was time to get this game started.

But then I stopped.

I set the ball on the ground, reached up, and took off Dad's hat. I freed my hair from the bobby pins and ponytail, and it fell around my shoulders. I put the hat back on, pulled my arm back, and let go of the first pitch, making sure to throw like a girl!

ACKNOWLEDGMENTS

In *You Throw Like a Girl*, Gabby finds a team that accepts her for who she is. I'm so lucky and blessed to have my own team behind me throughout the writing of this book.

So thank you, thank you, thank you to the following:

My amazing agent, Natalie Lakosil. I'm pretty sure selling a book less than two weeks before you have a baby and two weeks after your author has a baby is a first!

My editor, Alyson Heller. Yay to creating another book together! I couldn't ask to work with a better editor or a nicer person!

Thank you to the team at Aladdin. I'm forever thankful for all the magic you did to make this book what it is. And a special thanks to Dung Ho Hahn, who created the cutest cover ever!

My writing buddies and critique partners are the best! Thank you to The Lucky 13s and my Aladdin M!X girls. You always know just what to say to reset my confidence. And I couldn't have done this without Elle LaMarca, my Writing Soul Sister, Plot Whisperer, and the best Internet pen pal ever! Thanks for all your advice, cheerleading, and humor. I can't wait to go on our WSS-Around-the-World tour!

ACKNOWLEDGMENTS

Endless hugs to my family, who have supported my writing from the start. Thank you to the Alpine side, who have listened to me tell stories since I was young, and the Mielke side, who have welcomed and rooted for my writing every step of the way.

Thank you to my teammates and coaches at St. Angela, where so many fun memories were made while playing ball. I may not have been the best softball player, but I sure did love playing the game. And to my grandpa, who helped to instill in me a love of the Cleveland Indians. I have so many memories of sitting in the bleachers at Cleveland Municipal Stadium or listening to games on the radio. Cleveland is my city and the Tribe has also been my team!

A huge shout-out to my students and coworkers at Perry, especially Ann Rayner, Michelle Rayner, and Jodi Rzeszotarski. There is nothing better than sharing my love of reading and writing with all of you, and your encouragement and enthusiasm is contagious!

None of this would have been possible without my BFF, coffee! You pretty much run my life, so a special shout-out to my Keurig and the coffee shops who welcomed me (often for hours) while I wrote this book, especially the east side of Cleveland Starbucks, Panera, and Barnes & Noble!

ACKNOWLEDGMENTS

A million thanks to my awesome readers. You all rock! Writing middle-grade is a dream job, and I can't even begin to express how much I love you all.

My never-ending thanks goes to my husband, Jason. I don't think this book would have ever been written if it wasn't for you taking a colicky screaming baby every night from eight to eleven, so I could write.

And last but certainly not least, my biggest thank-you goes to my little dude, Nolan. This book was sold when you were only nine days old, so most of your early life was spent sleeping in your carrier at Starbucks while I consumed large cups of caffeine and wrote (as documented on Instagram with the hashtag #writingwithnolan). Thank you for being such a good sleeper! You're the greatest gift I could ever receive in life and inspire me to be the best person I can be. I love watching your story unfold in front of my eyes!

Here's a peek at another great story from Rachele Alpine!

It's pretty much impossible to get out of Mrs. Reichard's room during one of her history lectures. Many have tried, but few are able to claim success.

All my other teachers let you go to the bathroom if it's an emergency, but Mrs. Reichard is not like most teachers. She acts as if leaving her class is a personal attack on her. The woman drones on and on and absolutely refuses to let anyone get up and leave until she's done "filling your heads with my wondrous fountains of knowledge," as she says. Short of needing serious medical attention, you're stuck in her room until the bell rings. Actually, I'm not even sure calling 911 would work.

But today I had a mission. And I wasn't about to let anything stop me. Not even Mrs. Reichard and her "fountains of knowledge," because class was over in ten minutes and I needed to see the cast list for *Snow White* before anyone else.

I raised my hand as she babbled on about the settlement of the American West. She paused and lifted her eyebrows as if I were interrupting the most thrilling discussion ever (which, for your information, it was not. Not even remotely close. It looked as if half the class were trying to stay awake, and there was one kid in the corner who had lost the battle and was drooling onto his desk).

"Yes, Grace?" She peered at me over the top of her bright red reading glasses and looked positively peeved that I had the nerve to disturb her lesson.

"Can I go to the bathroom?" I wiggled around a little bit, hoping she'd get the idea of how important the situation really was.

But of course she didn't buy it.

"How about you wait until class is over," she said in a way that was not a question, but what my English teacher called an imperative sentence.

"I can't. This is an *emergency*," I told her, and squirmed

even more in my seat to make it seem like this was a life-or-death situation. Some of the kids around me giggled. My face flushed red, but it didn't matter. Let them laugh. I needed to complete this very important task, and time was not on my side.

"I don't see any reason why you can't hold it for the ten more minutes we have left in class." Mrs. Reichard turned her back to me and wrote some notes on the board.

"Please," I begged, even though this was getting downright humiliating. I imagined my classmates whispering in the hallway about how close I came to having an accident in history. They'd point and laugh and make up some awful nickname that had to do with diapers or something equally embarrassing.

She sighed so loud, I swear it shook the walls. "Go ahead, but hurry back."

"Thank you, thank you, thank you!" I shouted, and jumped up. I glanced at my best friend, Lizzie, as I raced to the door. She rolled her eyes, and I winked at her. She knew I was going to see if the list was posted. It always went up at some point during last period, right before the school day was over. Probably because our director, Mrs. Hiser, didn't want to deal with the drama from those who didn't get the parts they wanted. Mrs. Hiser was smart. Post it when everyone was leaving and our parents would be the first ones forced to listen to us complain, not her.

I learned the hard way how important it is to look at the list alone. Last year I thought I was going to get a lead role and talked about it the whole day. I checked the list with the rest of my friends only to discover I was cast as Snowflake Number Three. I wasn't even Snowflake Number One. The experience taught me that it's a lot easier to find out you got a teeny-tiny part when there aren't a whole bunch of people around you.

I rushed out of the room but slowed down to check and make sure the hall monitors weren't around. If they spotted you anywhere but the bathroom, it was back to class immediately, and I couldn't risk getting caught before I completed my mission. I used my ninja-like skills and moved through the hallway undetected.

Finally, I made it to the last hallway before the drama wing. As soon as I turned the corner, I instantly knew the scene I caused in class was worth it, because the list was up! The bright yellow paper hung in the center of the bulletin board. The palms of my hands started to sweat and my heart pounded. I approached slowly, and when

I stood in front of it, I put my hand in my pocket and pulled out my lucky marble. I closed my fingers around it and squeezed tight before I looked at the list.

Now, I'm not a superstitious person. I stroll under ladders as if it's no big deal, open umbrellas inside because it beats getting rained on when you have to do it outside, and if a black cat crosses my path, I'll bend down to pet it.

I don't believe in any of that ridiculous stuff. Nope. Not at all.

Until I audition for a play.

Then I turn into a person obsessed with the power of lucky charms, because ever since I discovered my magical marble, I've been cast in every show. Mom says I get the parts because I'm talented, and she might be right—and I've taken many acting, dancing, and singing classes—but I firmly believe that if I didn't have my marble, I'd be doomed to a life of stage crew. Not that there is anything wrong with stage crew, but why would I want to hide behind the curtain when I could be out front where I belonged, blinded by the bright lights shining on me?

I clutched my marble, closed my eyes, made a wish, and read the names from the bottom of the list to the top like I always do. It helps prolong the seconds I can imagine I might still have a chance at the lead. Sometimes the anticipation is better than the actual real thing, especially when the real thing means getting a part like Snowflake Number Three.

My eyes moved higher and higher, and I held my breath, hoping against hope I was Snow White. *Please let me get the part, please let me get the part,* I chanted to myself.

My friends Lizzie, Beck, and I had sat together in the theater watching each person audition, and they both pinkie-swore I was the best Snow White out of the whole bunch. I didn't say anything back to them, but I silently agreed. I rocked the audition. Usually I'm nervous before trying out, but not that day. I walked across the stage and said my monologue as if I had been born to play the Fairest in the Land. And now the time had come to see if all my hard work had paid off.

I found Beck's name and giggled when I saw he was Grumpy the Dwarf. Beck was the complete opposite of grumpy; I don't know if I have ever seen him in a bad mood. He would get to show off his acting chops with that role. Lizzie was on the list too, as a townsperson, which would make her happy. Lizzie was more of a small-role type of girl. I, on the other hand, most certainly was not.

I rolled the marble around and around in the palm of my hand as slowly, slowly, my eyes made their way to the top, and there, right at the very tippy-top, was my name.

Grace Shaw: Snow White

Me! Me! Me!

I couldn't help it. I threw my hands up in the air and danced. I totally busted it out in the middle of the hallway. A hall monitor stared at me, so I waved, because, really, what did it matter? I didn't care at this point if the whole school saw me breaking it down. It wasn't every day that a seventh grader got the lead in Sloane Middle School's play. Usually those parts were given to eighth graders, but not this time!

I looked at my name again and touched it. My fingers traced the letters, and I fist-pumped the air.

This was big! This was major! This was the best day of my life!